SOMETHING WICKED

6 Young Adult Paranormal Stories

Short stories by

Lena Brown
Heather Dearly
Mari Hestekin
Kelly Parra
Jenny Peterson
Aaron Smith

Edited by Mari Farthing

Buzz Books USA
Celebrating stories.

www.BuzzBooksUSA.com

Published by Buzz Books USA, an imprint of Athena Institute, LLC.

ISBN-10: 1938493060

ISBN-13: 978-1-938493-065

Trade Paperback Edition

Introduction

We're tipping our hat to the infamous quote by William Shakespeare and featuring the same fabulous line up from *Prom Dates to Die For,* plus one debut writer, Mari Hestekin.

In this collection, you'll get superpowers, a haunting, a mermaid, spiders galore, and even trolls. Back by popular demand, Kelly Parra and Jenny Peterson are continuing their stories they started in *Prom.*

While this collection is full of tricks, it's definitely a treat for readers of all ages. We hope you'll take the time to come tell us what you thought of it on our Facebook page, www.facebook.com/somethingwicked as well as sharing reviews on Goodreads and book retailer sites.

Thanks for reading and celebrating stories with us.

- Malena Lott, executive editor, Buzz Books USA

Table of Contents

Under Loch and Cay – Jenny Peterson 6
Arach War – Lena Brown 29
Through a Glass Darkly– Heather Dearly 46
Mermania – Kelly Parra 67
Midnight Troll – Mari Hestekin 90
Spectral Media– Aaron Smith 110
Author Bios 133

By the pricking of my thumbs,
Something wicked this way comes.
Open lock,
Whoever knocks!

-From Macbeth by William Shakespeare

Under Loch and Cay

by Jenny Peterson

"Perfect." Rachel Chase shouldered open her dorm door and grumbled at the perky alarm chirping from her phone. "I'm going to be late again. Just perfect."

She spared a second to tug her brown hair from its pony—maybe it'd look sleep-tousled? — but it kinked at the back of her head and fell limp. Yeah, or not. She looped it back into a high bun and shrugged off her canvas backpack. The pack was heavy, but she swung it easily into the back of her closet. It hit the tile with a thud and the dull clank of metal.

Rachel was nearly out the door before she stopped, groaned and turned back. With a sigh, she lugged the bag back out and pulled it open, reaching past wooden stakes and satchels of dried herbs for the blood-crusted dagger at the bottom.

Slowly, methodically, Rachel ran the silver blade under the tap and watched the black blood swirl down the drain. The sulfurous musk still stung her nose and made her eyes smart, but it was nothing like it had been two nights ago deep in the Blue Ridge Mountains when the tar-like blood had oozed over her hands and burned like acid.

Rachel was hopelessly late by the time she finally wiped down the clean blade. The thought of being late—again—made an ache bloom in her stomach. She was not the type of girl who missed class. Then again, she never would have thought she was the type of girl who had to worry about keeping her weapons clean.

Rachel locked her dorm room and ran. The courtyard outside was so silent Rachel could hear the wind rustling through the pines standing sentinel around the dorms. She strained to hear anything else that could be lurking in the hazy blue Georgia mountains surrounding Saint Etienne University, but she was alone. The humidity clung and caught at her limbs like a sodden wool blanket. Rachel swallowed a gulp of the still-thick October air and pumped her legs.

Finally, she skidded through a pair of heavy wooden doors. The history building's air conditioning slapped her in the face and raised goose bumps along her arms, but she kept running. She would not miss another class. She wouldn't.

The Ancient Civilizations classroom was up two flights of stairs and down a long corridor. Rachel planted her feet outside the final door on the left and pressed her hands to her chest as she listened to the murmur and rumble of class in session. Her heart thundered, but not from the run. Late again. Dammit.

Rachel counted to five in German and opened the creaking door. Down at the theater's podium, Professor Rathbone stopped and settled his mouth into a grim line. Every head in the class turned and stared.

"How wonderful of you to join us, Miss Chase."

"I— um, I ..." *You see, I was tracking a wendigo*

through the mountains and cornered it outside a cabin just as it was about to chow down on three hunters. Oh, you didn't know I hunted demons when I'm not in class? Yeah, that'd go over marvelously. Rachel pressed her lips together and knit her eyebrows. "I was studying and lost—"

"Please no excuses, just find a seat."

Rachel picked her way as quickly and quietly as she could past knees, backpacks and the flip-down trays sticking out of the chair arms. The heat of a hundred eyes crept up her neck and blazed in her cheeks. Why in the hell had she decided on Saint Etienne instead of a massive state school? That whole thing about being a name, not a number? Rachel would've given anything to be a faceless numeral at that second.

Rathbone waited for Rachel to sink into her seat before turning back to the young man standing next to him. "As I was saying, we're departing from the syllabus today to hear from Mr. Sidney Martin, who has been a research assistant on one of the archaeology teams studying the Lascaux complex. Xerxes will have to wait as we travel instead to paleolithic France."

Rachel cocked her head and frowned. *This kid* was a guest lecturer? He barely looked older than she was. And he was wearing a bow tie. It did nothing to make him look older, just a bit peculiar. Sidney Martin glanced up and caught Rachel staring. The smirk that curled at his lips sent Rachel's cheeks burning bright red. She bent over her notebook and started taking notes.

ᛉ

"So, this you-know-what ... did you ...?" Rachel's best friend Kendra bared her teeth, hissed, then mimed being staked through the heart. The kid behind her in the cafeteria line frowned.

"Totally subtle, Kendra."

Kendra shrugged and slid her caf card. "Rachel, my love, you have some sort of black ickiness down one leg of your jeans and you smell a bit of *eu de monster*. Now who's being subtle?"

Rachel looked down at her jeans and sighed. There had been a time when she didn't have to worry about walking around with demon blood on her clothing. Apparently that time had passed. She followed Kendra to an empty table and plopped into a chair.

Kendra prodded the sides of her neck–it had turned into a new habit in the last six months–before turning to Rachel. "Seriously, is our wendigo dearly departed?"

"Dead and gone, though it took me twice as long to track and kill the thing than I thought it would. It was past the Carolina border by the time I cornered it. Bastard made me late for Ancient Civilizations."

Kendra grimaced. "Rathbone strikes again. Are you sure he's not in the Corpus? I'm positive I saw something about terrible professors in there."

Rachel rolled her eyes, but grinned. Ever since she and Kendra had learned about their identities–Rachel as a line of demon hunters called Descendants, and Kendra as a half-mermaid–Kendra had been pouring through the Corpus, a lexicon of demonology, and memorizing the classification of each creature and whether to welcome, repel, or fight them.

Rachel stabbed at her salad. "He's obviously a predator." She lifted her fork like a dagger and speared "Professor Broccoli."

"That's lunch, Miss Chase, not my wendigo."

Rachel spun and dropped her fork. It bounced off the toe of a worn-in brown boot and left a trail of Italian dressing and broccoli bits. Rachel looked up—past the bow tie—into the face of Sidney Martin.

Rathbone's guest lecturer sat down like they were old chums, reached for Rachel's diet soda, and downed it. Rachel just watched him, wordless. It wasn't until he slid the empty can across the table she realized he'd said the word wendigo. But that couldn't be right. Maybe he'd said "I should go" or "Tupelo" or something. Rachel shook her head a tiny bit to clear her thoughts. When she looked back up, Sidney waggled his eyebrows and leaned back, hooking his fingers through the loops of his pants. He seemed entirely too pleased with himself.

Sidney smirked at Rachel then swiveled toward Kendra, but his smug grin instantly shriveled. His eyes bulged and he snapped up straight. Rachel cocked her head and watched as he held out a hand toward Kendra's neck, then pulled it back and scrubbed his hands through his dark blond hair. "I was not expecting gills on that one."

"That one?" Rachel's words came out in a growl.

Sidney rolled his eyes. "Calm down. I meant your friend. It's not exactly common to see a half-demon eating a sandwich with a Descendant."

"I'm half-mermaid, not half-demon." Kendra tried to keep the hurt out of her voice, but Rachel could still hear it.

He shrugged, oblivious. "It's the same thing, really. Ap-ple, *ahh*-pple."

"You mean po-tay-to, po-*tah*-to."

Sidney shrugged again, and the movement made Rachel's lip curl. "Sorry, English isn't my first language. It's my fourth language, actually."

"Wow. So, yeah ... we're gonna go." Rachel scooped up her empty soda can, but before she could stand, her phone buzzed in her pocket. She turned her back and answered the call from her mom, but Daphne Chase was looking for Kendra. She handed the phone to her best friend, who wandered over to a corner to talk, leaving Rachel with no choice but to turn back to the haughty foreigner now picking tomatoes out of her salad.

Rachel narrowed her eyes and leaned forward. "Can I do something for you, Mr. Martin?"

"Please, call me Sid." His accent was hard to place. It was somewhere between British English and something more continental. "And yes, you can tell my why you stole my kill."

Rachel didn't have an answer for that.

"That wendigo was mine," Sid continued. "I'd been tracking it for months through half of Europe and here to the States. I spent a week sleeping rough near the Loch of Cliff. Do you have any idea what the weather is like in October along the shore of a Scottish loch?"

"Chilly?" Rachel didn't know what else to say. This complete stranger was sitting across from her talking about a once-human demon that gorged on human flesh like he was chatting about last week's biology exam. It was unnerving at best. Sid fished another tomato out of her salad and popped it in his mouth.

Rachel pulled the tray of food out of his reach. "I take it you're a Descendant too?"

"I'm a Martin."

"Ooookay."

Sid scrunched up his forehead then sighed. "There really aren't all that many of us. I don't know how you could forget a name of one of the families."

It was Rachel's turn to frown. "There is nothing *to* forget. I don't know any of the other families. I mean, I just got my inheritance like six months ago."

"Right, the Chase women don't inherit until age eighteen. But didn't you wonder why you learned weapon training as a kid?"

Now she was really confused. Sid took one look at her, and his gray eyes went wide. "*Merde*! You don't know anything, do you?"

Rachel bristled. "I know *a lot* of things, just not all the Descendant stuff. But I'm learning fast." She leaned forward on her elbows and leveled her gaze at Sid. "How do you know who I am? And why did you show up pretending to be some Lascaux expert?"

Sid crossed his arms. "I know who you are because it's my job to know. And I didn't pretend; I really was interning at the site—until the wendigo showed up and started eating my professors, that is."

Rachel opened her mouth to ask more, but Kendra was back, and she looked worried.

"We need to talk," Kendra said, her mouth tight.

Rachel abandoned her food and followed Kendra out into the hallway. Sid trailed them, like a nattilydressed stalker. He cleared his throat as Kendra was unlocking their door.

Sid leaned against the doorframe. "I can give you valuable advice with whatever's going on here." He smiled broadly, like he was going for sweet and helpful sidekick. It didn't work.

"I have some advice for you," Rachel said. "Lose the bow tie."

Sid frowned. "I thought it made me look professorial."

"More like jackassorial. Seriously, you look like a character off of BBC."

Beside her, Kendra grinned and shut the door in Sid's face.

ᛠ

"Who *was* that guy?" Kendra collapsed back onto her bed and resumed Gill Exploration 101.

Rachel scooted to the back of her own bed and pulled her knees up to her chest. She sniffed. Kendra was right, she *did* stink. With a grumble, Rachel peeled off her soiled clothes in favor of something cotton and stretchy. She leaned a hip against the sink and turned toward her friend. "What did my mom want?"

Kendra sat up, her hands still at her neck. "She wants my help. There have been some accidents off Shipwreck Cay. Three boats capsized in the past week."

Rachel's hands flew to her mouth and her heart kicked over in her chest. Jake. He worked on his uncle's tourist boat. When was the last time she'd talked to her ex-boyfriend, a month? "Why wouldn't Mom—"

"No one's been seriously hurt yet. But three boats

in a week? *Something* is going on. Your mom suspects a predator, but she hasn't been able to get any more information." Kendra paused and blew a long, slow breath out of her nose. "That's where I come in." She paused again. "She wants me to try and talk to the merpeople."

Rachel's eyes went wide. "But have you ever ..."

"Never. But, I mean, I've got to try. It's almost the season-ender. That many boats in one place ... it could be a disaster."

Rachel crossed the tiny room and sank onto the edge of her bed. The boat captains, deckhands and most of the townspeople celebrated the end of the tourist season with a massive party on Shipwreck Cay every Halloween, which was tomorrow. That meant she and Kendra had a day to get home, track down some merpeople, and figure out just what was sinking boats. That shouldn't be impossible at all.

Rachel sighed and looked down at her pajamas then she reached into the closet for fresh jeans and boots. "We might as well get going then."

They were nearly done packing when someone knocked on the door. Rachel was bent over cramming weapons into her backpack, but she heard Kendra pad to the door and pull it open. Then she heard her groan.

"It's Monsieur Baguette," Kendra hissed, leaning close.

Rachel straightened up, already frowning, as Sid sauntered into their room. He had thankfully lost the bow tie, but he was carrying a battered duffle ... and a bow and arrow. The bundle of stakes in Rachel's arms dropped to the ground with a wooden clatter.

"What in the hell is that strapped to your back?"

Sid swiveled to show off the slender bow slung over one shoulder. "It's one of my favorite weapons."

"No," Rachel retorted, hands on hips. "It's Robin Hood's favorite weapon."

Sid rolled his eyes, and the motion made Rachel's nostrils flare completely on their own. "Robin Hood was nothing but a hanger-on. He—"

"Whatever. What are you doing here?"

Sid smiled wide. "I'm here to help!" Rachel narrowed her eyes, suspicious. "I had a nice chat with Daphne Chase, and she invited me along to help her daughter."

Rachel's nostrils flared again. "We don't need you to help."

"I jumped a cargo plane to get here. I haven't been home in three months. And then I don't even get to bag the beast? The least you can do is let me tag along."

Rachel glowered, but Kendra finally spoke up. "Fine. But we're leaving now. And I better not catch you staring at my gills."

The three of them were jammed hip-to-hip in Kendra's truck not an hour later. It was after midnight by the time she eased the old pickup into Shipley, but they agreed to meet at the docks by eight the next morning.

Jake sounded less than pleased when Rachel called at seven a.m. His voice was gravelly, and he didn't seem capable of speaking in more than two syllables at a time. Rachel resorted to begging.

"C'mon, Jake. Kendra needs to do this free-dive for class."

Rachel could practically hear Jake shrug though the phone. "Why haven't you called?"

Crap. Not this. "Jake," Rachel said as gently as she could. "We broke up. It was mutual. I don't know what you expect me to do." She didn't add that terror had gripped at her chest when she learned about the boats capsizing.

"Yeah, but ... but we ..."

Rachel sighed, and the line went silent. It was strange to think that less than six months ago she had been a straight-A student whose biggest worry was whether or not to lose her virginity. Now... She wasn't a straight A-student anymore, that was for sure. And that whole virginity thing? Lost. To Jake the weekend before she left for college—the weekend *after* they'd broken up—on the deck of his boat, of all places.

"Jake," she finally whispered. "Please?"

The wind blowing off the ocean had a frigid salt bite that gnawed at the bits of exposed skin at Rachel's neck and hands. Though it wasn't nearly as biting as the look Jake was throwing at Sid. Rachel cast Jake a warning look before bending her head close to Kendra, who perched at the stern.

"You're sure this is the spot?"

Kendra stretched in her slick black wetsuit and nodded. "That's what your mom said. Most divers can't even get close to the cave entrance, but..." Kendra's gills fluttered in the wind. She wasn't most divers.

Rachel shaded her eyes and stared out at the water of the deep cove. It was choppy and gray, but protected from the larger ocean swells. "Do you know what you'll say if you find them?"

"Don't eat me?" Kendra grinned, but there was a twinge of nervousness lacing the smile. Then she blew a big breath out of her nose, snapped her diving mask over her eyes and started taking massive, deepening breaths. It always made Rachel nervous to see her friend prepare to dive, but this was what Kendra loved. She took one final breath and jumped over the side.

Kendra would stay under twenty minutes, though she had once told Rachel she could probably go longer. It was against all safety protocol to let her dive by herself, but Rachel had convinced Jake to keep out of his SCUBA gear. Instead, her ex-boyfriend had folded his long body in one of the seats and was glowering at Sid.

"Who are you again?" Jake's voice came out like a bark.

"Sid Martin, a family friend."

"But you're foreign."

Sid pulled a half-smile. Rachel couldn't see his eyes behind his sunglasses, but she assumed he'd rolled them. "Well spotted! I'm French."

Jake snorted, like the whole of France had personally offended him. "You don't sound French. And I've never heard Rach talk about you."

"I attended an English immersion school, then a special boarding school in Norway. And I wasn't aware you knew every single person Rachel's family was acquainted with."

Jake stared for a long moment then got up with a snarl. "This is stupid to not have a partner diving with her, Rachel. I'm surprised at you." He pulled his wetsuit up over his arms and grabbed his snorkel gear. Without another word, he jumped into the water.

"He was pleasant," Sid said with a smile.

"Shut up."

Sid complied, and the next few minutes passed in awkward silence. Rachel finally spoke up. "Did you really go to a boarding school? Is that where you got that weapons training?"

Sid leaned back in his chair and stretched his legs out, propping them up next to her. "I knew you'd be the first to talk."

Rachel shoved his feet away and scowled, but Sid only laughed.

"Yes, I really did go to boarding school after I inherited at age ten. But I started my weapons training at age five."

Rachel's mouth dropped open. "But that's ... that's nuts!"

Sid shrugged. "For the families still in France, this is our lives. You know how we became this way, right?" When Rachel shook her head, Sid continued. "A thousand years ago, our village was beset by monsters, so the elders sought help from a coven of witches. They made a member of each of those village families special, and each descendant takes up the duty to protect humans and civilian demons from those who would prey on us."

"But my mom told me there were rules against telling us anything before we inherit."

"Technically that's true, but would you really want your child—your child who is born a target to certain demons—unprepared to defend itself? A lot of those first families dispersed across the globe. I've heard some have tried to separate themselves from their fate, but you really can't escape it."

From over the side of the boat, Jake spurted a stream of water out the top of his tube. "She's coming back up!"

Rachel tried to stand, but Sid reached out and put his hand on her arm. He leaned close and talked fast. When he did, his accent thickened. "If you didn't know any of this until you turned eighteen, and you never trained on any weapons, how did you kill that wendigo?"

The heat from Sid's hand crept through the layers of clothing, but she didn't pull away. Sid pulled his sunglasses off and leaned close, talking fast. His gray eyes were wide, and there was an earnestness in his voice. He pushed back the dark blond hair that fell over his eyes and stared at Rachel.

"I ... I stabbed it." She swallowed and pressed her lips together. How could she tell Sid that it seemed to come naturally, that she now had a strength and precision she couldn't explain? "It's weird, but I faced a succubus the night I inherited, and I knew exactly how to kill it."

Sid sat back with a long whistle. "That," he said, "is impressive."

Jake crested the back of the boat, droplets of water shining like a thousand diamonds on his wetsuit. He glared at Sid then turned to haul Kendra up. She was beaming.

"How was it?"

Kendra wrung out her hair and grinned. "Informative."

Kendra was close to bursting by the time they made it to her truck. In the ten minute drive back home, Rachel was fairly sure Kendra used the word "awesome" at least fifteen times. Rachel's cheeks hurt from smiling by the time they pulled up to her house.

"And this city! I mean, an honest-to-god city! They said I could come back any time and they'd show me around and just ... oh, Rach! It was ..."

"Awesome?" Sid supplied. Rachel threw him a look, but his face broke into a wide grin.

They found Rachel's mom in the greenhouse, and Kendra launched into her contact with the merpeople. According to them, a kraken had been seen hunting in the treacherous water off Shipwreck Cay. And a kraken this close to shore meant just one thing: "Sirens," Rachel's mom said with a heavy sigh.

She opened her Corpus with a groan of creaking leather and turned the ancient book so they could read. The page was labeled "predator," which meant it actively hunted civilians and was to be killed on sight.

Rachel ran a finger across the description. "Are these the same thing that hung out on shores calling to sailors?"

Her mom nodded. "Basically. They have a way of singing that lulls people into a trance. They're amphibious, but can't breathe under water, so they stick close to shorelines. They pull in the boats, and their kraken kills."

“What’s the point?” Kendra asked.

“Hearts,” Sid answered. “They eat human hearts, which the kraken delivers.”

Rachel shivered. “Lovely.”

Sid frowned. “The kraken is just a threat, though. They’re usually really solitary and only hunt in the deep, deep ocean.”

“Yeah,” Kendra said, nodding. “The merpeople said they wouldn’t kill the kraken, but they will help corral it.”

“The main priority is to find the sirens and keep those boats away,” Rachel’s mom said. “Sid, can you take the lead with the sirens? Rachel and I will try to hold up the captains.”

Rachel shook her head. “No, I want to fight.”

Kendra piped up. “Me too. How else will you know if the merpeople are successful?”

Rachel’s mom pursed her lips and frowned, but she finally nodded. “We have six hours until the boats will try to leave for the cay.” She pulled open the doors to the weapon shed. “Let’s get going.”

It was nearly sundown by the time they approached Shipwreck Cay in the boat Rachel had begged from Jake. All of the tourist vessels had capsized as they made the swing out around the western tip of the island, where jagged rocks broke the surface and lurked just below. Instead, Rachel veered well south and docked at a rundown pier.

Rachel jumped into the sand and started walking. There were scrubby hills, gnarled oak groves and grassy dunes between them and the other docks. She had her silver dagger through her belt and another four blades tucked into a sheath, and Sid had a dagger at each hip and his bow slung over his back, the gray feather fletching of his arrows sticking out of his quiver. Kendra had agreed to carry a curved blade, but she kept eyeing it suspiciously, like it might try to attack her at any second. Most importantly, they each rubbed a compound of dried juniper berries, crushed caraway seeds and powdered angelica root in their ears to ward off the siren song.

Sid heard the song first and grimaced. "It sounds like two cats mating."

The song grew louder—and Sid was right about the mating cats thing—until the notes shrieked in Rachel's ears. It sent shivers rolling down her arms each time a gust of wind buffeted against her, a horrible mix of salt tang and siren song.

The sinking sun burned her eyes, but she stared ahead, afraid even to blink. They were close, she could feel it. And hear it.

They broke through a curtain of Spanish moss dripping from the twisted oaks and nearly walked straight into them. From the edge of the crooked trees, the ground fell away in a tumble of grass, sand and giant driftwood logs. Below, seven sirens lounged on the ragged rocks thrusting up from the sand and sea, surrounded by the half-eaten carcasses of what looked like dolphins. Rachel swallowed back sour bile at the sight. The sirens had the raw form of women, but their skin was moist and pale, like something you'd uncover on the underside of a rotten log. One of the sirens stretched out an arm to soak it in the sea, and the failing light illuminated the blue veins worming under the skin and stretching across the translucent webbing between its fingers.

A sudden hand on Rachel's shoulder made her jump, and her dagger was raised in a flash. But it was only Sid. "What," she hissed.

He leaned close until his breath fluttered the fine hair escaping her ponytail. "Listen, you may find me arrogant or annoying or any number of things." Rachel snorted in agreement, but Sid went on. "No matter what you think, you need to know you can trust me in a fight. More than anything else, we're Descendants. We'll come through for each other."

Rachel opened her mouth, then closed it again. Sid squeezed her shoulder. "Okay?"

She nodded. "Okay."

Then without another word, he slipped his bow over his head, notched an arrow, and let it fly. Down below, a siren shrieked. Then the screaming began.

Rachel gripped her dagger and took two big breaths before she burst through the curtain of moss and ran. One of the sirens was down, black blood oozing from an arrow sunk into its chest. But six more came fast.

Rachel vaulted the giant driftwood that littered the ground and crashed into a siren. Its skin was eel-soft under her fingers and sticky with seawater. The feeling of it churned the contents of her stomach, but she set her jaw and slashed out with her dagger. The blade skittered across the creature's chest and opened a gash that wept thick blood, but the siren kept coming. Its face was crude, with no nose and fleshy lips that parted to expose blackened fangs. The siren shrieked, a horrible thing that shivered through Rachel's clothes and prickled against her skin. Then it snapped its jaw and sent the tangled strands of seaweed hair slapping wetly together. Rachel reached out and grabbed a hank of the slimy, green weeds and pulled.

The siren twisted away with a screech, but it didn't drown out the thrum and whoosh behind her. Fletching grazed Rachel's cheek, then an arrow lodged into the siren's throat. Rachel let go of the creature's hair just as the thing burst into a flood of tar blood and whipped around. Sid perched atop a driftwood log, his bow held taut.

"She was mine!"

Sid grinned, dropped his bow and pulled two daggers from his belt. "Now we're even." He jumped from the withered log and hurtled into a melee of three sirens. Rachel kicked against the wet sand and took off after him, but a terrible, terrified scream wheeled her around.

Two sirens stalked Kendra, slowly pushing her farther into the dangerous water. Kendra sobbed as she jabbed and swung the curved blade, but the sirens slid out of the way each time. Rachel watched in horror, her legs leaden with fear, as her best friend thrust wildly one last time, only to crash against one of the lurking rocks. She dropped the blade, and the water—her beloved water—tugged her deeper.

"No!" The shout ripped out of Rachel's throat. She raced over the wet sand and plunged into the water. One of the sirens pulled Kendra deeper among the jagged rocks as another ripped at her coat. Rachel crashed against the waves and dove straight for the closest siren. She grabbed the creature around the neck and hauled her off Kendra. With one, quick motion, Rachel sunk her dagger into the siren's back, felt it scrape again its spine then flung the dying creature away.

Kendra whimpered and started swimming desperately out to sea, but the last siren slipped after her. Rachel swam, the cold, dark ocean pulling at her clothes. She clamped her dagger between her teeth and struggled on, every kick a fight against the tug of the sea.

She yelled for Kendra, teeth barred around the cold metal dagger, but the girl was too frightened to hear. There was a horrible sucking sound, like water swirling down a drain. Rachel choked and sputtered as a single, monstrous tentacle rose out of the churning water and slapped the surface. Another surged upward into the purpling twilight and hovered, blood red and pockmarked with a thousand pale suckers. Rachel blinked stinging saltwater out of her eyes just in time to see another tentacle, this one slithering across the surface like a snake. She yelled, her voice harsh and raw, but it was too late. The tentacle curled around Kendra's arm, the siren wrenched at the other, and her best friend was gone.

Rachel dove, but the water was a riot of bubbles and movement. There was a flash of silver as her dagger sank out of sight and a streak of gold as something below her circled and thrashed. Kendra was lost in the pressing darkness, but Rachel grabbed wildly at the kraken and held tight. She wrenched one of her knives out and slashed at the squishy flesh of a tentacle. It writhed then stiffened, the meat under its skin rippling with corded muscles. Too late, Rachel tried to let go. The kraken punched her in the gut, and her lungs expelled the last of her oxygen in a jet of bubbles.

Kendra was gone. And then. That same golden brown swam closer. Through the black water it took shape slowly. First a long fish tail, then a broad torso, then a girl cradled in its arms. The merman pushed Kendra's limp body toward the surface and sank out of sight. Rachel shot up, her lungs burning, and gulped down frigid air as Kendra bobbed up next to her, coughing up seawater. She grabbed her friend under her arms and hauled her to shore.

The smell of roasting hot dogs and the sound of laughter wafted through the Spanish moss as Rachel, Kendra and Sid limped closer to the bonfire, covered in ichor and sticky with salt. Yet none of them could stop smiling.

Around the orange bonfire that licked at the edges of the night, boat captains donned masks and howled at the moon. Sparklers hissed and spit as deckhands raced past, and Halloween music curled around the revelers. Out to sea, the colored lights strung along the boats turned them into floating Christmas trees and blazed like beacons on the boats still drifting in. The line seemed to stretch all the way back to the fuzzy illumination that marked Shipley.

"God, Rach, what is it with me finding you covered in tar and smelly?" Jake pushed a werewolf mask up his forehead and wrinkled his nose. He grimaced at Sid and Kendra.

"Nice to see you too."

"How's my boat?"

"Yeah, we're doing all right, thanks," Kendra countered.

Jake ignored her and pulled Rachel aside. "Listen, I was hoping we could—" His nose wrinkled up again and he stuck his tongue out. "Seriously, Rachel, I can't even talk to you right now. You smell like a shrimp boat."

Rachel narrowed her eyes and glared. "You really know what to say to a girl, Jake." She turned away and grabbed Kendra and Sid by the hands. Without saying a word, she pulled them into the ocean.

Sid yelped when the water hit his stomach, but soon all three were bobbing in the dark water, the full moon on the horizon. It was almost warm under the waves.

"You know," Sid said. "You're pretty good with that dagger. I should teach you how to use two at a time. Double the fun."

Rachel pushed strands of wet hair out of her face and looked at Sid. Hair plastered the sides of his head and water beaded at his jaw, and in the reflection of the moon, his eyes seemed to glow. "Yeah," she finally said. "I'd like that." And she meant it.

"And after that, I'll make you a bow convert."

Rachel laughed just as something brushed against her bare feet. A second later, the head of a merman crested the surface, followed by a dozen more. Each had wild, tangled hair and gills at their necks. Each was smiling.

Rachel spun in a circle before alighting back on the merman closest to her. He had Kendra's lips and pointed chin, though his skin was darker and glowed a warm gold in the moonlight.

Under the surface, the merman pressed the familiar hilt of Rachel's dagger into her hand. "Thank you for being there for her," the merman said. His voice was rich and rolled over Rachel like music.

"She always has been," Kendra said, her eyes locked on the merman.

He nodded. "The kraken is on its way back to the deep." Then he slipped back under the waves along with his brethren and left Rachel floating in silence with Kendra and Sid at her sides.

Far out to sea, a massive tentacle arched above the waves and hovered against the moon. Then it splashed back to the water and disappeared.

Arach War

by Lena Brown

The wind whipped Athena's dark hair as she scurried down the rocky path between the library and the sorority house, books tucked into her chest, head bowed, over thinking as usual. Her timepiece told her she was late — as if the descending orb in the sky hadn't done it first. She cursed at the irony that she had received the new member punctuality award in the chapter meeting just three moons ago.

She wouldn't have time to go back to the dorm to change into a Halloween costume, nor have time for her sister, Aphrodite, whom they called Ro on Earth, to fix her hair. A light mist began to fall as the wind howled between the canvas of trees. If she had her powers, she'd wish for tiny wipers to clean off her lenses, but without them, she simply saw through the blurry water droplets and picked up her pace.

It wasn't that she hated parties, per se; it was that she was expected to love them. Just because she was, by human terms, a college freshman, did not mean she could change her ways, or a millennia of intellectual grooming. She'd rather think than party — but thinking would only get her so far on her mission, which was to understand these humans better, to become a better muse, which meant she and her real-life Greek sisters, Aphrodite and Artemis, were in this thing together, for better or worse.

Her vision blackened, only in her right eye, then the dark spot moved, crawling. She screamed, a rightly sissy scream, and jumped back as if that would separate her from the thing on her glasses, still on her face. In haste, she flicked the spectacles off, sending them spiraling to the stone as she stepped aside, feeling a creeping sensation all over her skin.

She felt ticklish brushes against her hand, her neck, and was unable to shake them off fast enough. Spiders, black as night, and the size of a quarter, had dropped from the trees, hanging from their silken rope. Not a dozen, but perhaps a hundred or more. After shaking off two, she spun around, trapped, unable to move in any direction without heading smack into one. She knew etymology —spiders come out at night and spin their web to catch their prey — but she had never seen them like this, so many of them, and not on the walk she took every evening. The library was more home away from home than the dorm or sorority house would ever be.

"Move," she told herself, but her legs wouldn't obey. She could call on help, but she'd left her compact back at the dorm. Any reflection enabled the goddesses and gods to communicate with each other, mirrors being the optimal channel.

The sun barely peeked over the horizon beyond Mid-America University, which meant if she didn't move soon, she wouldn't be able to see at all. She dropped to her knees and grabbed her glasses. One cracked lens from the fall, but the other was fine. She wiped away the moisture. This wasn't a job for Ro, the goddess of love and beauty, but Art, the huntress.

"I barely recognized you without your glasses," Art yelled over the loud music.

"Broke my glasses. I can barely see you. Where are you?"

"The frat party," Art said. "Where you're supposed to be. Are you wet?"

The spiders descended, inch by inch, an arachnid orchestra.

"I've got a slight situation. Spiders. Lots of them."

Art tossed her head back. "It's Halloween, silly. Humans love this holiday. Day of the Dead, which is why we're supposed to be on watch."

"Yes, about that," Athena said, her eyes on the spiders, "I'm wondering if Hades sent a legion of spiders."

Art laughed. "To scare a timid goddess? I don't think so. Now get your butt over here."

"Listen! To! Me! Look!" Athena turned the glasses around to show her sister the mob of spiders surrounding her. "Help!"

"Wow. You weren't kidding," Art said flatly. "You either belly-crawl out of the trees or you make a run for it and shake them off as you go."

"Seriously? That's your answer? Not coming to my rescue?"

"By the time I got there, who knows what might happen," Art said. "But you're going to see a lot of webs and spiders tonight. They use them as decorations! See?" Art spun her compact around to show off the frat house. Webs covered almost every surface, spotted by large plastic spiders. Except ...

"Wait! Go back! That one moved!" Athena yelled, but it was too late. Art had dropped the compact, leaving it on its side, a perfect angle to see the tarantulas, dozens of them, crawling out from under the furniture.

So much for a quiet Halloween, Athena thought, opting for the belly crawl through the grass, about forty feet, before she was clear of the trees, and scrambled to her feet.

It was the first time she understood what the expression "ran like a bat out of Hell" really meant.

At the intersection between the dorms to her left and Sorority and Fraternity Row to her right, she debated whether to go to the dorms to see if Ro was still there – Ro hated spiders even more than Athena did – or get to the fraternity house to help Art.

As a war strategist, Athena knew this called for something beyond reacting to the symptom. They had to get to the source. Someone had unleashed spiders on campus, and until she figured out who – and how to stop them – they'd all be doomed.

She needed a plan.

To the dorms she headed, popping out the broken lens so she could see out of her good eye and carefully avoiding the trees, which was nearly impossible since the beautiful campus was covered in them.

The streetlights flickered on, and with their glow, she could read the chalk messages on the sidewalk. The crude child-like drawing of a large spider caught her eye, with the message, "Welcome to the World Wide

Web!"

It could be nothing, she reasoned. As Art pointed out, this holiday brought out all the pranksters. In fact, the spiders could be one frat playing a joke on another. One *could* buy tarantulas at a pet store.

Only that wouldn't explain how many of them were in those trees.

She raced on, looking for more clues. Adams Hall seemed to move, but as she got closer, she saw that it was a mass of spiders, a sea of black racing up the brick. They were already to the fourth floor; the sisters' room was on the sixth.

Unable to snap her fingers and make herself reappear in her dorm, she swung open the security door and walked smack-dab into the center of a web, spun with human prey in mind. The more she moved, the more stuck she became, practically spinning a cocoon herself just by trying to escape.

Looking around, she noticed she wasn't the first victim. Three human cocoons were dangling from the rafters. Preening her ear, she heard their muffled cries for help. *Good, not dead. Yet.*

Unable to reach her glasses to call for divine help again, she did what mortals do: She screamed. The cocoons moved, swaying and twisting, letting her know they heard her. Only they couldn't help.

It seemed most of the occupants had already left for Halloween festivities. A strange ticking noise seemed to be coming closer. Looking up, she saw her own reflection — in the eyes of a spider the size of a Volkswagen Bug. No way that was natural. *Hades!*

With all her strength — which wasn't much beyond

a typical teen's — she plunged forward and released herself from the web and was able to turn and face the glass, enabling her to summon Ro.

Just as Athena suspected, Ro was still upstairs, curling her long tresses. "Ro! Are you okay?"

"I'm great, but what do you call that costume? Mummy goddess?"

"It's a web. No time to explain. Look, you're not going to like this, but you need to go to the roof, now! Hades has obviously put some spell on the campus and there are spiders everywhere."

Ro's peachy complexion drained to white. "Spiders? What size? How many?"

Athena rushed through the sliding glass door and it shut just in time to catch one of the spiders' legs. Its high-pitched squeal pierced the air.

"What was that long stick?" Ro said, dropping her curling iron.

"That was a spider leg. One of eight. And they are *all* that long! Do *not* come down the elevator! The big spidey is spinning cocoons of students. You have to go to the roof."

Ro shook her head. "You know I'm afraid of heights."

"Any less than you're afraid of spiders?"

"Good point. But how will I get down? They can still get me up there!"

Outside, Athena searched the perimeter for something, anything, to catch her. "A banner! I'll get some help and you can jump into the banner."

"For a brainiac, you've lost your mind," Ro said. "But as much as I appreciate your concern, you need to deal with the bigger issue. What does Hades plan to do with us all these students? You have to stop him. When I escape, I'll find you at the Delta Chi house."

Ro had already disappeared, most likely to take her chances with the stairs.

Athena raced down the sidewalk, again dodging the trees, and noticed more human cocoons hanging from stoplights, streetlights and limbs of trees. Anger filled her petite frame. She may normally be the "good girl" goddess, but tonight, all bets were off. First, she needed to find someone on campus who would know about Hades' plan.

Ever since the goddess sisters had come down to Earth, Hades had let a few from the dark side make the trip, too, beginning with his wife, Persephone. She spent the spring in Olympus and the fall with Hades, and he'd already sent her to try to keep the girls from pledging a sorority. Or could it be Eris, who had sent the evil note before school started that she was looking forward to a reunion? No doubt, the dark holiday had opened the door between the worlds. But spiders didn't seem like Eris' weapon of choice; she was far from a nature lover.

Athena picked up her pace, running down the sidewalk toward the frat house, when she gasped at the shadow of herself merged with that of a spider: half-woman, half-spider. She spun around and saw that the spiders chasing her were the size of dogs, yet their shadows had made them look much bigger.

"Arachne!" she yelled.

How had she not thought of it before? Thousands of years before, Athena and Arachne, a princess, held a weaving contest. While the mortal was a gifted weaver, her tapestry was a slap to the gods, depicting the infidelity at Olympus, including many sins of Athena's own father, Zeus. Enraged, Athena had destroyed Arachne's tapestry and cursed her to live in extreme guilt for what she'd done.

Arachne responded by hanging herself. Filled with remorse, Athena brought Arachne back to life, but cursed her again — to live as a spider.

"How did you come through and plan all this?" Athena asked the wind while barely outrunning the legions of spiders headed straight for the very party she was going to.

A thinker by nature, Athena could barely hold on to her thoughts on the run. Where would Arachne be on campus? She'd need a space big enough to weave, but someplace where she'd be protected.

Envisioning the map of campus in her mind, she went through several buildings until it hit her: the football stadium. Yes, Arachne could be on the field while her spiders protected her at all the entrances.

How would she get to Arachne without being spun into a cocoon? The stadium was blocks away. Even if she got a ride to the stadium, she'd need to be lifted over it to avoid the spiders. But how?

Stopping in her tracks, Athena ran across the street into the Gamma Lambda parking lot and attempted to open car doors until she found one that was unlocked. She fumbled through the glove compartment. Nothing. The car smelled of beef jerky and beer. She reached under the seat and felt something, pulling it out. A keychain, clutched by a spider. She threw it against the glass of the passenger door, killing the arachnid. The key dropped to the seat.

The car started, but the fuel light blinked orange: empty. No time to get gas. She peeled out of the parking lot, running over the curb in the process. Zeus had thought it better not to let the girls get a driver's license, but since Athena read everything, she had read several driver's ed books, just to see what she was missing out on. She swerved through the streets, gunning the gas, and running over spiders. She heard the squish beneath her tires and the squeal of spiders. *Did they know her?*

Spiders jumped on the car, covering the windshield. She turned on the windshield wipers, sending some spiders flying while others were flattened, their insides smeared onto the glass.

"Eww!" she yelled, trying not to pay attention to all the other cars and their inhabitants, already covered in webs. Several larger spiders had started making their way across her car, trying to trap her inside, even while it was it motion.

She grasped the rearview mirror. "Artemis, are you there?"

Arts' image appeared in the rearview mirror.

"Just a sec, Sis," Art said, putting the compact in her teeth, showing the arrow leave her bow, followed by the sound of a splat. The hunter goddess had to be loving this. She was in her element.

"Why aren't you here?" Art asked, looking back at the compact.

"No time! I think Arachne is finally getting her vengeance!"

Another curb.

"Are you driving?" Art asked.

"I couldn't find anyone not already cocooned to give me a ride! Stay with me, Art! I need Helios to bring his chariot and take me into the stadium by air. I think that's her lair," Athena said.

Art shook her head. "I don't know. He just finished taking the sun across the sky. If he brings the chariot, he may not have time to make it back to start the sunrise."

"Oh, Art! I know very well you've been sneaking out of the dorm at night to see him on the rooftop!"

Art smiled. "Fine! You got me. But he usually rides Pegasus. He takes out a big loan to the stable to bring her this far."

"Whatever! I'm willing to make a deal, with him *and* the stable owner for all I care. From the look of things, we're going to need all the help we can get."

"I'll see what I can do." Art snapped the compact closed.

Athena realized she'd been driving with the headlights off, and when she switched them on, she couldn't help but scream again. The spiders were much thicker the closer she approached the stadium. They were starting to gum up the motor, while some of the smaller ones tapped at the air-conditioner vents, trying to break their way through. The windows were nearly covered in webbing, but the moon was bright and she had less than a block to go to reach the stadium.

When she arrived, she circled the stadium to look for a way in, just in case Helios couldn't – or *wouldn't* – help her. All the gates were padlocked, and besides, they were covered in spiders. The car sputtered, with barely enough gas to go another few meters. In one last attempt, she drove through a smaller gate in the practice field as the car sputtered to a stop.

All the stadium lights were on, revealing how quickly the campus had been covered in webbing. By tomorrow, MAU would be no more.

Using a biology book in the passenger seat, Athena killed as many spiders as she could, trying to keep her eye out for a chariot or winged horse. Finally, a flash of something crossed the lights above the stadium and landed with a thud on top of the car.

A horse whinnied. Helios had come.

"Watch out!" Art's voice yelled from above, as she pierced the roof with an arrow. With Helios' help, she ripped the top off the car, and pulled me up. The breeze of Pegasus' flapping wings above caused our hair to fly in all directions. She hadn't seen Pegasus in years, since one of Aphrodite's famous Ambrosia parties; taking rides on Pegasus was always a hit.

"Thank you," Athena said, breathless.

"I was planning on seeing her tonight, anyway," he said, putting his arm around Artemis. "But you still owe me big for Pegasus. She's more expensive on holidays."

"Just give me the price if – when – we make it through this," Athena said. "Let's go!"

Helios leapt to mount the horse, and reached down to grab Athena's arm, pulling her up atop Pegasus.

"What about you?" Athena asked her sister, who was fiddling with her arrows.

"I'm Plan B," Artemis said. "I have some nets. I've got your back. You know I'm the fastest runner in track and field. Just go!"

Pegasus, her beautiful white mane glowing in the dark, took off as Athena wrapped her arms tightly around Helios' middle. His golden skin glowed.

"You talk to Achilles in a while?" Helios asked.

Athena bristled upon hearing Achilles' name. The one god who turned her mind to mush. "Let's focus on our mission, shall we?"

"That's our war strategist!" Helios said with a laugh as Pegasus sent them over the stadium. A gorgeous tapestry, only two-thirds complete, covered the structure's left side: An image of Athena and her goddess sisters as half-spiders were weaved in a long line of MAU students, also transformed, and paying reverence to the spider goddess, Arachne. She was planning on turning them, not killing them.

Arachne looked up from her tapestry, noticed them, and hissed. Her legs were long and human; her body a bloated, shiny-black torso with a large head atop it. Her mortal eyes sat beneath six glossy spider orbs on her forehead.

Pegasus landed gently on the tapestry. Helios jumped off and helped Athena down.

Arachne skittered over to them, hissing all the way. "Look what the horsie dragged in," she said as she raised two arms. "Trick or treat!" she cackled.

Athena crossed her arms. "I wish I could say it's nice to see you again, but it's not. Let's talk about this logically."

"Logically?" Black liquid seeped from Arachne's mouth. "What's logical about what you've done to me? Why didn't you let me stay dead?" She pointed a hairy finger at Athena, just inches from her face. "This is all *your* doing."

Helios stood beside Athena, ready to break Arachne's arms if need be, but he wouldn't get far before the thousands of spiders around them would attack.

"I get that you're upset," Athena began, but Arachne pushed Athena down into the tapestry and crawled over her.

"No! You don't get to talk to me about feelings! You have no idea what it's been like to be all alone, a freak, for all this time! The only thing that kept me going was to find the perfect plan of revenge. But you were so protected on Olympus, I could never break in. When your father sent you to Earth, I knew I had to find a way to cross into this world. That's when I talked to a few of your favorite enemies and found out today was the one day I could visit – and with the help of a curse, I conjured the aid of the arachnids."

"Who's helping you?" Athena demanded, wiping the dark goo from her face that dripped from Arachne's mouth.

"It doesn't matter! By the time my tapestry is complete, it will be midnight, the witching hour, and everyone in the cocoons will emerge as half-human, half-spiders! I think we'll start a sorority of our own. How about AGD? Arachnid Gamma Delta!" She laughed wickedly. "We'll get those silly party shirts and everything!"

Athena shook her head. She couldn't outrun her, but she could outthink her.

"That's not what you really want," Athena said with

a small smile. "You came here because you miss being a mortal. But since I was the one who placed the curse on you and changed you into a spider, I'm the only one who can undo it."

Arachne backed away, looking affectionately at the spiders around her. "Why would I turn my back on my kind? Spiders have welcomed me into their community. You couldn't stand that I was a better weaver than you! It was your ego that got in the way!"

"Fine! You want me to say it? You're a better weaver than I am! But you *have* to understand something about gods and mortals: we don't want our indiscretions thrown in our faces! The world is judgmental enough. I can make you a mortal again and you could be the best clothier on the planet, but use your skills for the greater good! And I know you can do better than party shirts."

Arachne folded four of her arms, pacing. She walked over to Helios and placed a hand on his shoulder.

"I wouldn't mind seeing the likes of mankind again," she hissed. "I kind of like it here. I want to be young and beautiful again. Make me a college student at MAU."

"It's a big world," Athena argued. "Pick another university. Anywhere but here."

"Spiders!" Arachne yelled, and they began finishing the tapestry furiously while she pinned Athena back down.

Athena rolled her eyes. "Wait! You can stay," she conceded.

"That's not all. I want to be your sorority sister. As

they say, keep your friends close, and your enemies closer."

Great, Athena thought. *Her curse has boomeranged back.* Not only would she have to put up with Arachne, but she'd have to be extra-nice to her because Arachne knew her secret identity.

"Fine. If you return everything to the way it was," Athena said, wanting to bite off her own tongue, "then I'll work up the paperwork to make you a transfer from another university and you'll be in my house. We'll call you Rachel."

Arachne pondered it. "Let me talk to my partners in crime and see if what has been done — or in this case, spun — can be unspun."

She skittered away while Helios helped Athena to her feet. In the distance, Artemis waved her golden bow in the press box. Helios commanded Pegasus to pick Art up and bring her back.

When Art returned, Helios helped her off the horse and kissed her.

"Oh," Art said, as if noticing Athena for the first time, "you were right: Arachne did have some help. I saw her crawl under the stadium. She's in cahoots with Eris."

"The goddess of discord," Athena said. "I figured she had something to do with this. That means Arachne will be indebted to her to make this all go away."

"Which means she's going to want something from us, too," Art added.

Arachne jumped back up on the tapestry, a wicked smile on her face. "It's been settled! The spiders will retreat to their homes. The webs will blow away in the wind and no one outside of us will have any memory of what transpired tonight. Just as soon as you've done your part."

"What's she talking about?" Artemis asked, her bow cocked.

Athena reached out and lowered the bow in Artemis' hands.

"Art, allow me to introduce you," she said, as she snapped her fingers, "to Rachel, the newest fashion design major at Mid-America U. And my ... sorority sister."

Arts' mouth dropped open as the trio watched Arachne transform, six of her legs retreating into her body, her black shiny coat turning to peachy human skin, the coarse hairs turning whisper-soft. Two eyes, not eight.

All around them, the web and the very tapestry they were standing on began to dissipate. Cocoons dropped and cracked open, students emerging as if nothing had happened, and headed back to enjoy the rest of their Halloween night.

"What do you say we go meet some sisters?" Rachel asked.

Athena groaned, and then donned a fake smile. "It's your lucky night. We're having a costume party with our frat brothers. But you'll need a costume."

Rachel shook her head. "I feel like I've been wearing one for the last thousand years. Why don't we just grab a witch hat and call it good?"

"Sounds about right," Art said, mounting Pegasus. "It's the one night Helios can dress as he is and fit right in." She hugged his middle and set her cheek against his golden shoulder. "Catch you later. Get it, *catch*?"

And Pegasus was off, leaving Rachel and Athena staring at each other.

"Shall we?" Athena asked.

"I thought you'd never ask."

The spiders made way for the pair, leaving a clear path as the new sorority sisters walked across the football field and out into the Halloween night.

"Do you think Achilles will be there?" Rachel asked as they neared Fraternity Row. "I used to have a major crush on him."

Athena resisted the urge to tell Rachel to back off, to leave Achilles alone. She knew Rach was just saying it to upset her, to test her, to try to start a new kind of war. Dating Achilles would make Athena jealous, and Rachel knew it.

"Oh, he's all yours," Athena fibbed. "I have a thing for someone else, though he doesn't know it yet. He's the quarterback on the football team. A real guy's guy. But you probably wouldn't have a chance. All the girls want him."

"Is that so?" Rachel asked. "We'll see about that. I know a thing or two about catching men in my web."

The music swelled as they opened the door to the frat house. Witches and warlocks, vampires and devils danced inside.

Tonight, everyone was good at pretending.

Through a Glass Darkly

by Heather Dearly

The earthbound spirit of a 10-year-old boy with bloodstained hair watched as I sat on the worn cobblestone of the crossroads. His face was shadow and sadness trapped on a tortured canvas, but his eyes grew bright and wide with the "gimmes" once I placed a handful of red cinnamon bears in the center of my freshly drawn design.

"Do you like candy?" I wiped my hands on my jeans as I stood.

"I did." He spoke in past tense. It was a good sign.

"Do you know why you're here?"

"Yeah. I'm lost, and I wanna go home." His focus shifted from the bears to me.

"And where is home?"

"I think it's in the light."

"Have you seen the light?"

His shoulders slumped forward in disappointment.

"Yeah. I didn't go into it, and now it's gone."

"Well, my name is Mia Vargas, and I happen to know someone who can show you where the light went. His name is Papa Legba."

"Is he your dad?"

"No. The Papa is not my father."

"Is he an angel?"

"Kinda. He's a Loa; a mysterious spirit very much like an angel or a saint, and he loves candy." I stuffed the half empty bag of bears back inside my pocket.

Papa Legba prefers sweets, coffee, or cigars as offering, but I would've settled for a brand new box of tissues. Souls will find me no matter the season, and they couldn't care less about the pollen count or my need to sneeze. Not that I expect compensation—I'm not a Voodoo Loa. I'm just a girl trying to survive her senior year of high school by avoiding grave mistakes—be they social, scholarly, or supernatural—and using my jacket cuff as a snot rag would be a totally gross display of social graces, or lack thereof, thank you very much.

I was working against the weather in an olive green zippered hoodie, a vintage t-shirt, a sterling silver crucifix, faded jeans, and pale pink sneakers. I never leave home without some kind of jacket and necessary supplies, because traffic between this world and the next leaves ethereal trails of mist and frost in its wake. As a gatekeeper of this realm, it pays to be prepared.

Plus, it keeps me from freezing my tiny ta-tas off.

Another trick of the trade is replacing the corn meal or flour I usually use to make my Vévé—a symbol used for summoning (rhymes with pray-pray)—with dustless chalk on days with strong Texas winds. I also opt for the weight of extra large cinnamon bears, which I acquire from the local Tractor Supply checkout aisle.

"A spirit with a sweet tooth?" His expression changed from worried to curious.

"You wanna meet him? I can come with." I stifled a

sniffle and smiled.

"Are you dead, too?"

"No, but it's okay, because I help people like you all the time."

My face grew numb as the temperature dropped below freezing when a brilliant, blinding light appeared in the middle of the road. I suddenly looked as pallid and putrid as the dead child—my skin shifting from smooth and dark to withering and light—but the kid didn't notice. I offered him my hand, and felt the brush of his unearthly fingers against my palm. Moments later, the brave boy walked into the light. I stood shivering in the road alone, staring at my Vévé; the uniform lines of its cross-like design unbothered by the wonky weather.

As usual, the bears were gone.

Still feeling chilled, I walked to my pickup. I wanted to thaw in my sun-warmed truck (a necessary precaution) before ordering a drink (to go) from the restaurant on the main road. My quivering, ice-kissed lips weren't a surprising sight to me in the rear-view mirror, but the drive-thru attendant at Bobby's BBQ would probably faint if she saw my complexion transform from corpse-like to normal. I don't like to advertise my abnormalities, so I soaked up every ounce of heat available. I also wiped my nose with a crumpled coffee house napkin before shifting from park to drive and returning to life.

No sooner than I'd paid for my strawberry soda, the sound of shattering glass made me jump from my seat. In an empty parking space to the right of the order lane, I saw colorful shards sparkle on asphalt in the fading sunlight. The lot was vacant of patrons, and was too far away from the road for the blast of glass to have come from there. I scanned the surrounding cars and trucks, but they were all empty.

Then I looked up and saw it.

A bottle tree.

I couldn't believe what I was looking at hidden behind browning leaves, and my mind raced for answers. Who was responsible for having hung blue bottles on the inner limbs of a Sawtooth Oak? North Texas was not a hot spot for Afro-Caribbean tradition. I lived in the buckle of the Bible belt, not New Orleans. Bottles trees have their purpose, definitely, but why would someone want to trap evil spirits this close to the crossroads?

The car behind me (oblivious to the significance of the scene) honked, and I promptly pulled forward and parked.

And then I prayed for blue, hoped against green, and braced myself for purple.

Voodoo tradition teaches that bottles trap the bad seeds of the spirit world, but that's only a partial truth; pure spirits who miss their chance to walk into the light can be attracted to shiny glass as much, if not more, than any evil spirit; and only those with eyes trained to see otherworldly phenomenon can verify if a bottle is vacant or occupied.

When it comes to spirits, yellow is positive (good) and red is negative (bad), so different colored bottles display different colored spirits. If a spirit trapped in blue, sun-soaked glass is pure, it glimmers green iridescent streams of light; it emits the dark purple shadows when it's not.

Purple bottles scare the crap out of me, so I needed to put on my big girl panties and act like, um, someone other than my scaredy-cat self. It was really important I get a look at the unbroken bottles in bright sunlight; light I was losing with every minute wasted hiding in my truck like the cowardly lion.

*I *do* believe in spooks, I *do* believe in spooks. I do, I do, I do...*

With courage falsely gathered, I got out of my truck.

The drive-thru traffic remained steady, so my brilliant plan was to walk over and sit on the sidewalk underneath the bottle tree as if I were waiting for someone. I couldn't exactly stand and stare, because that would draw too much attention to a potentially purple situation, but before I could take my first step toward the tree, an employee of the restaurant beat me there with broom and dustpan in hand.

And holy wow was he hot!

I watched the "too cute to be a busboy" sweep glass as I caught sight of something hanging from a leather cord slide out the collar of his shirt. He tucked it back in faster than I could flinch. It was a gris-gris (rhymes with free-free); a voodoo amulet that protects the wearer from evil, or brings love or good luck. I had no way of knowing what magic was used to make his, but if I had to bet, I'd put my money on protection from evil, which was a helpful (yet unfortunate) guess considering I'd lost too much light to see inside the bottles for myself.

I'd have to return before the restaurant opened

tomorrow. Joy.

Playing supernatural sleuth was not the way I'd hoped to spend my Saturday.

My original plan was to spend the day hunting for bargains, not clues. Abuela Vargas would have a heart attack if I paid retail for my wardrobe, and as she is the only family I have left, I shop smart. I don't want to be responsible for sending a 90-year-old Dominican Voodoo Queen six feet under, so depending on how much of a time suck my detective work proved to be, I was looking at a possible reschedule.

It didn't help that my window of shopping opportunity was already slim thanks to the autumnal equinox, but I wasn't about to ditch my plans with Abuela on the day of equal night. Not even for new shoes. Abuela's annual ritual for the souls of the dead would begin at sunset tomorrow—with or without me. I'd sooner die than leave her alone to honor what we'd both lost, and I refused to leave her and her hand tremors alone in the backyard with an army of lit candles.

Losing her or the family house was not an option.

I drove home, ate dinner, and fell asleep soon after; a sleep where I dreamed about the wearer of the gris-gris. In my dream, I watched him carry bottles in an old milk crate to the tree near the parking lot. Hoping to learn something new, I approached and asked him what he was doing.

His eyes—frightening and enticing—startled me awake.

I saw a storm brewing inside them.

I left the next morning before Abuela could grill me about where I was going. I hate to lie, and I especially hate to lie to her. She can't help that her dishonesty detector skills aren't what they used to be, so taking advantage of Abuela is something I try to avoid.

Deceiving grandmothers makes for bad juju.

It was half after seven in the morning when I returned to the restaurant. Sunlight was at an ideal brightness, allowing me to see through snug branches for a glimpse of telltale color. There were six blue bottles, one green bottle, and one purple bottle.

No bueno.

I slid the green bottle from its limb, capping it with a cork to contain the spirit. I did the same—even more carefully than the last—with the purple bottle. I gently wrapped them both inside a thick, soft blanket, and placed them on the floorboard of my truck in such a way to secure them against damage and me against danger. I broke the remaining six bottles.

Broom and dustpan boy could handle the mess. I'd deal with him later.

The good spirit would be set free at the crossroads. The bad spirit wasn't going to be so easy. With absolutely no field experience in the proper care and handling of evil entities, I had to make certain I could do so without screwing up. I wasn't going to pass a problem over to my best resource without having done my homework first, though.

Fingers crossed I wouldn't have to bother Abuela with any of this.

I returned home before she awoke. I carried the blanket-wrapped bottles to my room, cautiously setting them on my bed so I could close and lock the door behind me. Francis—our geriatric white and black cat—was sleeping on the padded lid of my hope chest, his favorite spot. His eyes opened in prince-like protest as I moved him from the lid to the window seat, but he closed them soon after.

I stared at the chest a long, hard minute before reaching for the lid.

The scent of cedar-infused sorrow filled the air as I moved memory books and dried funeral flowers to make room for the two spirits. The good, the bad, and the blanket were going to have a snug little slumber party in my hope chest until I could return with answers and a course of action. I covered the pile with a wedding shawl.

Closing the lid on my parents was always more difficult than opening it.

As I exited my room, I saw Abuela rattling around in the back of the house. I made my way to the kitchen to cook her *mangu con tres golpes* for breakfast (mashed plantains with fried cheese, salami, and eggs), and she managed to slice the cantaloupe without losing a finger. I cleared the table when we were finished, and kissed the creases on her forehead before telling her I needed to do some research for a project at the local library—which was partially true, but not really.

"I hope you find everything you're looking for, my little *mija*."

"Me, too."

I crossed myself and prayed for forgiveness upon

closing the front door.

I made it from point A to point B without getting a speeding ticket.

When I seek answers, my first thought isn't a building full of books—it's the cemetery. I trace the name Vargas with my index finger, searching for truth inside ridges of missing marble. I climb trees when no one is looking, and scan the rows of buried bones.

I cry at the feet of stone angels and saints.

St. Patrick. *Damballah.*

St. Jude. *Ghuede Gran Bwa.*

St. Peter. *Jan Bakéo.*

St. Anthony. *Papa Legba.*

The patron saint of lost things and missing persons, St. Anthony is associated with Papa Legba for good reason; practitioners consider him a miracle worker.

And I was going to need a miracle to fix this situation without my abuela.

"Shouldn't you be at the library?"

I nearly transported out of my skin as I turned around to find myself staring into the electric blue eyes from my dream. I immediately grabbed the gris-gris hanging from his neck, and zeroed in on the name embroidered on the breast of his black work shirt.

"You have some explaining to do, *Mason.*"

We were standing close enough for me to smell warm cinnamon on his breath and wonder if he smelled crisp melon on mine. He grabbed my wrist, forcing me to release the amulet. Slowly stuffing the cord back inside his shirt, he loosened his grip, but not by much.

"We'll get to that soon enough, *Mia*, but let's take a walk first."

He let my arm drop to my side, sliding his hand inside mine as if it belonged there. Mason's hold on me was firm, but far from threatening.

"Give me one good reason why I should go anywhere with you."

"Easy. You need my help."

"I don't know you, and I don't need you."

He winced at my words.

"Not only do you do need me, but we're running out of time."

I realized I needed more of a social life, because I'd be willing to bet his evening plans didn't include a date with his grandmother.

"I know why I'm running out of time, but why are you? And before you answer that, how do you know my name? And how in the *hell* do you know I'm supposed to be at the library?"

"I'm a client of Ruth Vargas."

I fell silent. The only other living souls in Abuela's daily life are the home health care nurses, my small circle of friends, and our next door neighbor, Paula, who takes her to Sunday Mass; all of whom have no idea sweet Ruth is a modern day Marie Laveau.

Abuela was a humble Voodoo Queen, not a famous one.

He had to be lying.

"And how exactly did you come to meet my abuela, Mason?"

"Walk with me, and I'll tell you."

His expression was absent of malice, but laced with

a prickly pain that pierced through me upon making meaningful eye contact. Common sense should have told me to say no, to turn away. Instead, inner wisdom urged me to face his divine white face and my fear of revealing the true me to the living. No matter how skillfully I'd convinced others that the only thing different about me was the color of my skin, the truth was there was nothing common about my private, peculiar life.

Ordinary was never going to happen for me.

So I went for a walk; a short one.

We stopped in front of a low-budget grave marker on the opposite side of the cemetery, and he released my hand. I stared at the final resting place of a 6-year-old girl named Cassandra Bell. She hadn't been in the ground for very long. Fresh, scarlet camellias filled her plastic memorial vase, the scent of intense sweet twisting the moment out of sorts.

"Mason ..."

"What?"

"Is your last name Bell?"

"Yes. Cass was—*is*—my sister ..."

It was my turn to wince. I was all too familiar with losing loved ones.

"She's also the good spirit in one of your bottles," he added.

"Wait—" My eyes shot wide open. "What do you mean *my bottles*? You were the one who placed them there, right? I saw you taking care of them."

"And I saw you take them. I need them back, Mia."

"No! I want to help your sister. I can help Cass cross over. I'll even let you be there when she does, but

I can't give you the other bottle. It's not safe."

"I know it isn't safe, because I know who's in the other bottle."

His voice was calm and determined with a side of scary. If this other spirit had anything to do with his sister's death, I could only imagine what he might want to do with it.

"That's even worse, Mason. You can't let whatever feelings you harbor against an evil spirit to fester. It will only give it power. I suggest staying as far away from the bottle as possible. Let me get rid of this spirit the right way."

"And how do you plan to do that, Mia?" He arched an eyebrow and crossed his arms, waiting for me to give him an answer.

Busted.

"I'm still trying to figure that out. I didn't want to involve Abuela, but it looks like she's already more involved than I am. I guess she's my—er, *our* only option."

Wondering why she chose to keep me out of this little loop of critical information made my stomach turn.

"I'm sorry Ruth is tangled up in this mess, but she approached me. I'd never even met her until my sister's funeral. I promise."

Abuela made first contact?

"I'll follow you home, Mia."

His words registered, but I didn't move. I was still trying to process why I was hearing all of this from Mason instead of Abuela.

"And we kind of need to hurry. Ruth is expecting us."

It was close to lunchtime when we arrived. Mason followed me up the front steps, but waited for a formal invitation before entering our home.

"You are not an imposition, child. Please come inside," Abuela said.

Three bowls of *Sopa boba*, a loaf of French bread, and a pitcher of ice water had been placed on the kitchen table. Abuela only cooks light, meatless meals when one of us isn't feeling well, so she obviously knew I would be returning home with a worried tummy.

Shame on her for keeping secrets!

I abandoned my gracious Texas etiquette as soon as everyone was seated.

"I'm not touching this soup until you spill the beans, Abuela."

"I'll tell you what you need to know, but first we eat."

Ignoring our exchange, Mason sliced the crusty roll with a chef's knife—my face a troubled reflection in the blade. His bowl was empty before I could blink, and he finished his second serving as I finished my first. I carried our dishes to the sink, rinsing them off as Abuela wrapped up what remained of the loaf in aluminum foil.

The doorbell rang.

Mason left us in the kitchen—in *our* kitchen of *our* home—and answered the door. After having asked for and being granted permission to enter, he was behaving as if he lived here, and Abuela didn't seem to mind one bit.

The ringer of the doorbell was Darlene, one of Abuela's nurses from the home health agency. She cradled a large canning jar containing what looked like a pink, jellied potato in her arms as if it were a fragile baby. Clearly distraught, she didn't even make an effort to acknowledge me or Mason before making her way to Abuela.

"I did everything you asked." Darlene spat out as she handed the jar to Abuela.

"It's time to tell Mia." As carefully as she could, Abuela carried the jar into the living room and situated it in the center of the coffee table for everyone to see, as if it were a vase full of freshly cut flowers. Mason and Darlene sat next to each other on the loveseat, and Abuela settled in the adjoining recliner. I stood beside an empty chair that faced them all, staring at what I realized actually resided inside the jar: a human heart.

"Tell me that's not what I think it is."

"It is what it is, Mia. Sit down and let us tell you why." Abuela was calm, yet spoke with the authority I would expect to come from a Voodoo Queen when addressing pressing (and possibly illegal) matters. I reluctantly seated myself in the chair.

"Please tell me we aren't dabbling in black magic, Abuela."

"We aren't dabbling in black magic, Mia. We're helping innocent people in need."

Darlene reached for Mason's hand, and I noticed they shared the same exhausted expression. They also shared the same blue eyes, blonde hair, and fair complexion.

"Cassandra, my daughter and Mason's sister, passed away recently after a long battle with leukemia. Their father, Michael ... well, he wasn't a good man. I granted him supervised visitation with Cass near the end, but it wasn't enough for him, so he showed up on our doorstep uninvited. Mason intervened when it turned ugly. Michael struck Mason, and Mason struck back. Michael fell and hit his head."

"It was an accident, but I killed him. I killed my father."

His voice cracked, and I felt awful for him.

"Is he the bad spirit inside the bottle?" I asked.

"Yes."

"And the heart?"

"Is what must be exchanged to make things right, Mia." Abuela rose from her chair, and walked over to the china cabinet where she stored her special supplies. She returned to the recliner with a spell kit.

"You asked them for his *heart*?!"

"It wasn't like that," Darlene declared. "We didn't cut it out ourselves. I have a friend who works at the coroner's office."

I blinked. Speechless, I turned my gaze back to Abuela.

"His dark spirit hovered above them both at the funeral and followed them home. I don't want Darlene and her boy to suffer anymore than they already have, so we are going to help send these spirits to where they belong before sundown. I'm going to vanquish Michael in Darlene's presence, because it's my responsibility as Queen. Mason will take you to release Cassandra at the crossroads, because it's your responsibility as gatekeeper. We will honor the dead together tonight."

I was *so* not cut out for dealing with evil spirits.

I rose from the chair and walked to my room in silence, closing and locking the door behind me. My life had just reached a new level of bizarre, and I thought it best to regain my composure in private. I retrieved the wrapped bottles, and lifted them gingerly from their makeshift hidey-hole. I placed the bottles on my bed before closing the lid of my chest for the second time in one day.

I gathered supplies and my last pocket pack of tissue and stuffed them inside my gray crossbody bag. I returned to the living room, and set Michael's bottle next to his rotten heart. I was glad to be rid of it. Darlene took the jar and handed Michael's bottle to Abuela, but tremors tricked her hands before they could make it out the back door.

Adrenaline flooded my heart.

The bottle's release looked like a lifetime supply of plum eye shadow gone boom in our kitchen—the powdery fallout a thick whisper of wicked pissed that only Abuela and I could see. Michael enveloped me, clouded my lungs with a fine paste of hate.

I grabbed the chef's knife from the sink.

Everyone dropped to the floor but Abuela.

This time, the reflection in the blade was of a much younger me covered in bloody cuts from windshield glass on the night of *the crash*. Little orphan me pointed at the expanding purple mass—she wanted me to kill it. I wanted to kill it, too. I wanted to steal this moment from evil the way fate had stolen every moment ever missed with my parents.

My arm swung a high right, my handle-gripped fist facing heaven.

Abuela pulled items out from her spell kit faster than I could stab, vanquishing Michael before Darlene and Mason could process how a canned heart could catch fire.

I dropped the knife.

My face flushed in embarrassment, in horror.

"Darlene, would you be a dear and help me clean up this mess?" Abuela massaged her hands as she looked toward me and Mason. "What are you two waiting for?"

"Oh, I don't know ... for my heart to stop racing, maybe?" I said.

She placed a now steady hand on my heart.

"This too shall pass, Mia. It always does."

Mason asked to drive, and I didn't have the energy to argue.

We arrived at our destination without me offering directions, which left me to wonder what other information Abuela had shared freely with Mason. Standing at the locked gate, I handed him Cassandra's bottle so I could dig the crossroads key out of my bag. An invaluable antique, it looks nothing like my truck and house keys.

"If I were a ghost buster, I'd peg you as the key master."

"Close, but no cigar." I tossed the key back inside my bag, and shut the gate behind us once we entered.

"Crap!"

"What's wrong?"

"I left my jacket in my truck."

"It's the middle of September in Texas. Why would you need a jacket?"

"You'll see."

It was a small comfort to know Abuela hadn't told him everything, but I suddenly realized I would need to explain a few things before I began to keep him from freaking out. Hopefully, a boy who wasn't fazed by the sight of his father's heart in a jar or a knife-wielding maniac wouldn't be too surprised by what happens when I help the dead.

"What can I do?" he asked.

"Hold on to Cassandra until I ask for her. I'm going to summon a spirit to open the gateway and allow her to cross over, but once you hand me the bottle, I need you to leave the road and wait over on the grass. I'm not sure what you'll be able to see, but I can promise you it's going to get, um, *weird*. I'll let you know when it's over."

I pulled a stick of chalk from my bag and got to work. Yesterday's Vévé had faded from the morning dew, so I traced over the lines to make them visible. I dumped the remaining bears from the half-used bag in the middle of the design.

"You can give me the bottle now." He handed Cassandra to me and distanced himself once he was confident I wouldn't drop her. His concern was wasted, though, because when I uncorked the bottle she wouldn't exit willingly. My only option was to throw the bottle outside of the Vévé, so I did. It exploded into miniature, blue bits of broken glass. Cassandra appeared unscathed by the experience, but Mason paced in his space like a nervous tiger.

"Can he see me?" She looked at her brother, but he didn't acknowledge her.

"I don't think so. I know he wants to, though."

I explained to Cassandra in kid-friendly terms what she needed to do. As soon as she understood, I began to freeze. She crossed over before I could say good-bye.

I picked up my bag, and gave Mason a frosty thumbs up.

And then he ran to me.

I looked like hell frozen over and he ran *to* me, not *from* me.

I knew my appearance would be a lot to digest, so he probably wanted to take me back home as soon as possible and be rid of me. I couldn't blame him.

"Are you okay?!" He wrapped his warm arms around me, and gave me the biggest bear hug I'd ever received in my life. I was totally shocked.

"I'll be fine. It just takes a few minutes," I said through chattering teeth.

"I thought you were going to die."

"Seriously, I'm okay." I lied. I was more than okay inside his arms.

"Did Cass—was she scared?"

"No. She walked into the light like a brave little girl."

When Mason let go of me, he picked me up and carried me to his car. He lowered me into the front seat, leaned over me to start the car, and turned the heater on for me.

"I'm not crippled, Mason. Just cold." And extremely flattered.

"You're welcome, Mia." He smiled a crazy, beautiful smile that made me melt inside, which wasn't an easy thing to do considering the circumstances.

"Thank you."

Mason's gris-gris slipped out of the collar of his shirt, and dangled in front of my face like a hypnotist's watch. The scent of juniper, rosemary, and something I couldn't place was almost as strong as the magic Abuela had used to make it. I could feel the charm's power as much as I could smell her rootwork. No wonder he kept it hidden.

"I guess you won't have to wear this thing anymore now, huh?"

His fingers brushed fondly against the amulet for a brief moment before tucking it back inside his shirt.

"Ruth told me if I kept the charm close, not only would it protect me, but that every beat of my heart would lead me closer to what I was looking for. I'm kind of afraid to take it off now that I know it works."

I hope you find everything you're looking for, my little mija.

And suddenly I placed the scent I'd missed: willow—the conjurer's gift. Mason's charm wasn't only made for protection; it was also made to attract love and good luck. Abuela wasn't dabbling in black magic at all. She was playing matchmaker.

Mason hovered between me and the open car door as I continued to thaw.

"Hey! I just realized you're wearing your work shirt."

"Almost forgot. I was distracted by a pretty girl. I should probably call in sick."

"I was supposed to go shopping today, but a cute boy messed up my plans."

"Sounds like trouble. He should apologize."

"He really should."

Mason didn't hesitate to show me he was sorry.

Warm, slow, and sweet ... I accepted.

Mermania

by Kelly Parra

Oz moved potion ingredients in a circular motion through the air with magic. A metal bucket of liquid stuff sat bubbling below on a cast iron stove. We were in Oz's War room. Not a battle-to-the-death war *room*, but war as in short for *warlock*.

"Wait, was that a rabbit's foot or a rat's foot?" Oz pushed his glasses up the bridge of his nose and the rat's foot fell to the ground.

Blake murmured in my ear, "Should we duck for cover?"

"I heard that, my boy!" Oz bellowed.

I smothered a laugh. Last month, Oz had mixed up a formula and blasted us, and every inch of his War room, with neon green slime. I was pretty sure it had to do with old age. The guy said he was 120 but he didn't look a day over 50. Old or not, he was as close to a parental figure Blake and I had. In fact, he was our magical mentor. He'd taken us off the streets when we'd been labeled freaks for being different, and not understanding why. Blake had been with him a little over a year, and me about ten months. I never understood how he'd known what we were. Oz didn't exactly go into specifics that he didn't feel were important. I mean, was there some magical mark on our foreheads only warlocks could see?

"What are you staring at?" Blake wanted to know.

"Just seeing if there was something about you that hints you're a magical detector of magical beings."

"A symbol for Supernatural Hunters?" Blake's lips curved. "And?"

"Not unless that big zit is any indication."

Hi hand slapped his forehead. "Where?"

"Relax. Your pretty boy face is still intact."

He rolled his shoulders, regaining his composure. "Funny girl."

"Why so nervous? Got a hot date?"

"No." He scratched his neck with a finger. "Just meeting a friend."

My mouth opened. Closed. Then, "Oh, who?"

"Someone from school. I think she has a case."

I lifted my eyebrows. "Should I come with?"

"Nah, I'll see if it's anything."

I returned my interest to Oz. "Fine."

"All right, what's been up with you lately?"

"What do you mean?"

"You've graced me with a little more attitude than normal. Some days you're distant. Some days you're nosey as hell. Like I said, weird. Is this a girl thing?"

I jerked a shoulder. "Don't you got a hot date?"

"It's not a date. Stop the pouting."

"I'm *not* pouting."

He flashed that irritating grin, and walked toward the front door. "Okay, I'll just ignore that bottom lip that's sticking out. Hey, Oz, borrowing the Caddy! Back in a bit."

"Yes, yes," Oz shooed him with his hand. "Where was that rabbit's foot? Jaz, deary, could you find me a rabbit's foot?"

I cringed. "Where?" But I knew.

"Over in the pantry, of course."

"Last time I checked for something in there, I discovered a very angry tarantula!"

"My dear, you face down evil supernatural beings that could turn you into troll turds, and you're afraid of a little spider? Tsk, tsk."

Resigned, I opened the pantry. "Wasn't little," I muttered. Painted mason jars were aligned on shelves. Putrid scents filled my nostrils. "Pig spit. Witch's wart? Gross. Bat teeth. Fairy toenails. Here, rabbit's foot." Hesitant, I opened the jar and a white rabbit's foot floated on air and over to Oz. Thank goodness. Sometimes Oz mislabeled.

"Thank you, my dear."

"Sure." I closed the pantry. "Hey Oz ... "

"Hmmm?"

"What happens after you've trained us completely?"

"When you become full-fledged adult supernatural hunters?"

"I guess. Yeah."

"I imagine you and Blake will go your separate ways into the world, continuing your destinies."

"Right. Separate. And you'll find new prodigies?"

"The cycle must go on. People grow older. Good must continue to fight evil. It's the balance of things."

Yeah, cycles went on, as did lives, people left even

when you didn't want them to go. Or they didn't love you like you secretly loved them, and they went off on dates with other girls. The grandfather clock in the hallway chimed ten and I couldn't sleep. Irritated, I got out of bed and stomped to the kitchen for some water. Of course, Blake wasn't home yet. His date must be really going well.

Goody for him.

So maybe I *had* been acting weird. Was that some kind of supernatural crime? *How are you supposed to act when you know you love someone and he doesn't love you back? Sometimes I tell myself to play it cool. Sometimes I forget. Sometimes I don't know how to act.* I squeezed my eyes shut. No wonder he questioned me.

"Will the real Jaz please stand up?"

When I moved to the sink, I cocked my head. Music, a soft whisper of melody that seemed to float outside on the evening air. I scanned the yard through the small window. Where was it coming from? I slipped into my mud boots, stepped out the back door and into the cool, starry night.

My hesitation dropped away like a veil, opening my mind to the most beautiful music.

I followed the soothing sound down the hill, and through a hillside of trees. Twigs and autumn leaves crunched beneath my boots. The night misted with fog but it didn't matter that my hair dampened or that my thin T-shirt stuck to my skin. The moon was nearly full.

The hike from atop Chapel Hill to the bottom was a long one. But time didn't seem to matter. The melody pulled me toward the lake and toward a rocky cove.

And there I set eyes on him. A boy a little older than my age of sixteen. In the water to his waist, playing a flute. Oddly, he wore no shirt, and his alabaster skin glowed under the moonlight. The flute was rocky with coral and shells. A smile seemed to touch his eyes.

I sat on a rock and listened to him play the last few wistful notes.

"I'm glad you came," he said.

"The song ... it's beautiful."

"What's your name?"

"Jaz."

"Jaz, you're gorgeous."

I laughed. "Sure."

"I said you're gorgeous ... do you believe me?"

And suddenly, I did.

"It's a nice night for a swim. Will you swim with me?"

It's cold.

"It's not very cold at all once you get in."

"Okay."

I slipped off my boots and socks, then my sweats and T-shirt. I stood on the rock in my underwear and bra, and stepped into the lake. A shiver swept up my body. Slime was under my feet and slippery rock. I swam to him into the deeper waters.

His arm came around me, holding me afloat. His features were what Oz would call angelic, with light colored hair, almond shaped eyes, a straight nose and full lips. He pulled the band from my hair and my black strands spread across the water surface.

His eyes were dark. When I looked into them, I

could see the reflection of the waters. So deep ... in his eyes.

"You're special, aren't you, Jaz?"

"No."

He closed his eyes and breathed in. "Yes, I can smell it. The magic." He met my eyes once more.

"Yes, I'm different."

"My name is Sotos. Say my name."

"Sotos."

"I want to kiss you. Do you want to kiss me, Jaz?"

"Don't think so."

He smiled. "I think you do."

"Yes," I said, my words breathless.

He leaned in, slowly, and pressed his lips to mine.

His lips were cool, soft. He pulled me tightly against him. His lips pressed harder. I nudged back. His hand came to the back of my head.

This was wrong. Not right.

Something sharp on my tongue.

Blood gushed.

Fear speared through me.

And together, we went under.

Cold.

I was walking.

But I didn't know where.

My body shook with chills. My teeth chattered.

I held damp clothes clutched to my chest. My feet were in boots but I didn't remember putting them on.

Something bright shined from behind me. A pair of lights. A car.

"Jaz! What the hell!"

That voice. I knew that voice.

I turned.

He grabbed me by the shoulders. His eyes were wide. Frightened. "What happened to you?"

When I just stared at him, he shook me a little. "Jaz, talk."

"I-I. Don't know."

He pulled me against him and hugged me. Abruptly, he let go, pulled off his sweatshirt and put it around my shoulders. "You're soaked and freezing. Let's go." He guided me to the car.

"Where?"

"Home. To Chapel Hill." He slammed the door and rounded the hood.

"You're Blake," I said when he got in.

He shut his door and swerved quickly onto the road. "Who the hell else would I be? Give me answers, Jaz."

"I can't."

"What the hell are you doing walking around in your freaking underwear?"

"I can't remember ... anything."

"What the hell was I doing walking around half-naked?"

"That's what I'd like to know," Blake said.

My arms were crossed as I paced back and forth in the War room. The brain fog I'd been feeling for the past hour had lifted. But there was a big black hole in my memory and I couldn't recall anything after Blake had left earlier that evening.

Oz was flipping pages of an ancient book. When that didn't give him what he wanted, he grumbled under his breath, and picked up the heavy tome, then dropped it on the floor with a thud. Next, he heaved another old book onto his desk. Dust scattered and he sneezed.

He rubbed at his pointy nose with a handkerchief. "Only a few magical creatures can take away memories. Vampires—"

Whirling toward him, my hand flew to my neck. "Vamps!"

"—use glamour to make humans see or believe anything. Blake, check for vampire bites."

Blake stepped toward me and removed my hand from my neck. He turned me left, then right. "Not seeing any."

"We'll need a full body scan."

"Get over yourselves!" I screeched.

"That you may do yourself, Jaz."

"Gee, thanks."

"Fairies and witches can conjure up spells to glamour humans. Or there are Merpeople."

"You got to be kidding me." Blake spoke up fascinated. "You mean like Mermaids?"

"Oh yes, my magical boy. There are many mystical creatures in our world. They used to roam the Earth without concealing themselves but once the written word began to document their existence and they began to be preyed upon by norms—and of course by hunters like yourselves—all mystical beings began to hide to save their well-being."

"Trippy."

"We are near the Harvest full moon. I will take that in to account in my research. Desiree is fixing some soup, Jaz, go ahead and eat before you rest."

"Yeah, okay."

Blake walked with me down the hallway. He touched my elbow. "You sure you're okay?"

I put on a brave face. "Hey, I don't break. Remember?" Blake had told me once that's what he'd liked about me. Truth was, heck yeah, I broke. And right now I was scrambling to try and find the pieces.

He brushed a strand of hair away from my cheek. "I say we stick together until we find out what happened. I don't want you taking off again by yourself."

"Don't you have a case?"

He shut his eyes for a brief moment. "Damn it, I forgot. I think she really needs help. It's sounding like a haunting."

"Filed under H. While you focus on that, I'll stick close to home."

"Home is where I left you, Jaz, and *this* happened."

His blue eyes looked concerned. I felt like going into his arms just to feel safe. But I had to remember Blake thought of me as a mouthy sidekick, and well, we were friends. *Best* friends—but nothing more. He didn't have the feelings that I'd discovered for him when he pretty much died in front of me at the hands of a soul-sucking Dark Angel.

Besides, if he'd wanted me on this case, he'd have brought me along in the first place. Obviously, he *liked* this girl.

A subtle ache throbbed in my chest.

"So what's her name?"

"Amber."

"What's she look like?"

"Why?"

I shrugged. "Curious."

"Blond. Kinda cute. Light brown eyes."

"Really."

We moved into the kitchen drawn by the comforting scent of chicken soup. Desiree's strong hands stirred a big pot on her stove. "Almost ready, Jazzy. Get yourself out a can of tuna for a sandwich."

"Thanks, Des." I grabbed a can out of the pantry and pulled out a can opener. I glanced at Blake while I opened the tin. "What are the clues?"

Blake leaned against the counter beside me. "Whispers in her ear. Lights flashing."

"Physical contact?"

"Possible shoving."

My eyes widened. "Freak out."

"She is." Blake moved to grab the bread and mayo from the fridge. When he turned to look at me, he froze.

I glanced at his weird look. "What?" I said with a mouth full of tuna.

His Adam's apple bobbed. "Good stuff you got there?"

I licked my fingers then looked down at the can. Not tuna. I'd opened a can of sardines and eaten half of the little fishes without realizing.

"UGH!" Slapping a hand to my mouth, I shoved out the backdoor and had a good gag fest.

Jaz.

I jerked up in my bed. Heart pounding.

Jaz.

I gazed around my dark room. No one was there. My heart pounded too fast. Sweat broke across my forehead.

My stomach rumbled. Then pain speared in my gut. So harsh, I bent over, gasping.

Feed, Jaz. You need to feed.

I stumbled out of my bed. "Help," I whispered. Could barely speak. Something tore into my stomach. Clawing. Tearing.

Feed your hunger ... now.

I shoved to my feet and out of my room. Blake's room was closest. I pushed open his door. He lay on his bed in the dark. I could hear his soft breathing. Could smell him ... he smelled of forest and pine, with a sweetness I could never describe. And underneath the rich tang of blood.

A tremble coursed through me. Hungry. So hungry.

Feed. Now.

I pulled myself upright with his bedpost. I fell next to him on the bed.

"What? Jaz? What's wrong?" His voice was sleepy. Disoriented.

"Blake, need ... you."

My heart pounded. Pounded. I reached for him. I pulled myself to him. His lips were a breath from mine.

"Jaz ... "

And I kissed him.

He kissed me back. The hunger slashed through me

like a knife.

NOW.

I pulled back. Fangs shoved through my gums and I hissed at him.

"Jaz!"

I jerked awake on my bed. Heart pounding. Breaths gushed from my mouth. My nightclothes were damp with sweat. I felt my teeth. No fangs. Normal.

"Dream. Just a dream."

I swallowed hard. Sank back into bed. Pulled the covers to my chin and waited until morning.

Amber was on the school swim team. After school, we watched her practice from the bleachers of Westside's High indoor pool. Now Blake had Amber cornered, asking her questions about the supposed haunting. She wasn't just cute. She was stunning. Slim with all the right curves, and she blinked up at Blake like he was just as hot to look at. Which he was, but still. I wasn't in the mood to listen to Amber fawn all over him. *Blake, you're so smart. Blake, can you help me, please? Blake, you're so brave.*

Gag.

I walked to the pool and dipped my fingers in the water. Nice.

Ten minutes later, Blake dragged me out of the pool area, soaking wet.

"You just felt the need to take a swim, Jaz? In your clothes?"

"At least, I didn't take them off this time."

"Hey, kid! You a student here?"

I turned toward a tall, female teacher, wearing sweat pants and a Westside High T-shirt.

"Yeah, took a quick dip. Won't happen again." I didn't think.

"What's your name?"

"It's Jaz, and I'm leaving."

"Jaz, I haven't seen a student have that kind of breath control and swim that fast in a long time. You've had training and you've got potential. I want you to try out for the swim team."

"Sorry, but no thanks."

The coach's lips thinned. "That's a real shame. Come find me if you change your mind. I'm Coach Landry."

When we were seated in Oz's Caddy, I locked gazes with Blake. "There's something wrong with me. I've never had training and the best I can usually swim is the doggy paddle."

Blue eyes serious, he nodded. "I know." He started the car. "Don't worry, Jaz, I'm not going let anything happen to you. We're going to get to the bottom of this."

I closed my eyes, trying to believe him.

"Stick out your tongue, Jaz," Oz prodded. "Be a good girl."

"This is dumb."

"My dear, you're the one walking around in your skivvies, eating little fishies, and jumping into pools on a whim."

I stuck out my tongue.

Oz peered closely with his ancient magnifying glass. First one side, then the next. He sighed as he pulled away. "It's as I suspected."

"What?" Blake and I asked in unison.

"You've been bitten, infected with DNA most likely by a merman looking for his mate."

"On my tongue?"

"What does it mean for Jaz?"

"If we don't help her soon, she'll turn into a mermaid by the next full moon."

"Can you protect her? How do we stop it?"

"I'll have to do some research. It's not every day, we come across—"

"Why the hell don't you know, Oz? Aren't you some world-class warlock? Aren't you here to train us? Keep us from turning into the supernatural freaks that we hunt?"

Mouth agape, I stared at Blake for his outburst. His cheeks were red. His shoulders moved up and down. He'd never spoken to Oz that way. In fact, I'd never even seen him flip his lid like this ever. I swallowed hard and glanced at Oz.

Oz ran his hand down has red braid and went to stare out his window. "You're right, my boy. I should be protecting you both better than this."

"Oz," I spoke softly. "We knew the risks when we signed up. Magic is dangerous. We were born hunters. The supernatural can sense us. If we didn't agree to our destinies, they'd find us and kill us, anyway." I turned to Blake, who wouldn't look at either of us. "Blake, you know that too."

Considering Blake had found me walking around half-naked when this all started, we went to the closest water source. The lake at the bottom of Chapel Hill.

"You sense anything?" Blake asked, quietly from behind me. He hadn't said much since his outburst with Oz.

"Not sure." I sat on the edge of an old pier, swinging my feet. A memory tried to surface. Water. Music? But then my head started to hurt. "It's all blank. I can feel some lingering power." And something else ...

"Me, too. But too faint. According to old lore, mermaids lure norms with a call from a magic flute that can hypnotize the victim. That must have been what got you down here. Jaz, what is it?"

I rubbed at my forehead. "My skin, it's tingling."

He rushed to me when I stood. "Uh ... don't do anything crazy."

"I'm hot." I pulled off my sweatshirt.

"Crap, not again. Keep your clothes on!"

I shuddered.

Blake gripped my arm, tugged. "Let's get out of here!"

Something splashed from in the middle of the lake. Blake and I zeroed our gaze toward the sound. A large, scaled tale splashed into the surface. Sunlight glinted off the scales flashing glimmers of rainbow.

"Holy ... "

"Merman," I murmured.

A male head popped through the surface. He bobbed in the water and stared at me with his cat eyes.

"Sotos," I said.

"Who?" Blake demanded.

Need to go to him. I yanked away from Blake and ran toward the end of the pier and jumped into the lake. Swimming into the cold depths.

"Jaz! No!"

A splash came from behind me.

I was too quick for Blake. I dove deeper toward the one who summoned me and swam farther away from the one I loved.

As I swam, heat rushed through my body even though the lake felt freezing. I began to strip my clothes away. Gnawing pain speared through my gut, then rocketed through my body in all directions. I cried out. Foul water rushed through my mouth. I gagged, swallowing. My legs fused together. Next, my fingers. Within me, bones jerked in directions I didn't think possible. My skin prickled and something scratched through the pores of my legs.

So much pain.

I must be dying ...

Suddenly all pain ceased.

Everything grew calm.

I could see clearly. Rays of sunlight beamed down into the water. I could hear the surface swish above me. Sense the fish and bottom dwellers at the bottom of the lake.

Peaceful.

Blake called for me. He splashed from far away.

He needed help. Needed me. Fear catapulted through me.

Blake couldn't swim!

I swam toward him.

Jaz.

Sotos called for me. Something inside me urged me to go to him.

Blake ...

I fought the compulsion and swam for Blake.

Once I spotted him in the distance, relief settled within me. Someone pulled him from the depths and onto the pier. I bobbed my head through the surface.

Amber. She'd saved Blake.

She helped him to his side as he coughed up water.

Blake finally stared in my direction. "Jaz, don't leave me! Jaz!"

My heart broke because I knew it was too late. I dove under, flicking my tail as I floated away to my new destiny. To my new life.

As a mermaid.

~

I had webbed skin between my fingertips.

Under the full moon, on a rocky cove, I slid my hand down the scales of my tail. The texture felt surprising soft and fluid. A real freaking tail! I was officially part fish.

Trip out.

Looking up at Chapel Hill, I wondered what Blake, Oz and Desiree were doing right now. I could barely make out the roof of the Victorian house.

I would never see them again. Swallowing hard, I blinked back tears.

"You could take your covering off now," Sotos spoke from the water.

He was talking about my bra. "You wish."

"You will leave behind your human ways soon enough."

I shook my head. "Why did you even choose me?"

"My flute called to you, Jaz. And when I felt your magic, I knew the flute had chosen well."

"Aren't there other mermaids you can hook up with?"

He smiled, but sadly. "There are no longer many of us. Kings and queens have hunted us for centuries as prizes. We have been brutally treated and often killed for our magic. Many times by hunters like yourself. This is how we survive."

"I'm sorry." And I meant it. Just because they were what fairy tales were made of didn't make it okay to be hunted and killed. "But still, you shouldn't take people against their will and turn them. It's what makes you evil."

"Does it?" He swam closer. "You must feed soon. Or you will not survive at all."

I did feel weak. But when I remembered my dream, I shook my head. "I will not feed like that."

"You will, Jaz."

His compulsion weighed down on me. "Don't—"

"You will feed, won't you, Jaz?"

"Yes, I will."

Sotos pinned down the old fisherman on the canoe. The little boat rocked. Soto's compulsion was like a heavy blanket of suffocation. Pain throbbed inside my stomach. I pulled myself onto the canoe, trembling with hunger. Sotos sucked from the man's arm, blood dripping down his mouth. My fangs slid from my gums.

Jaz, feed now!

I gripped the man's arm. He smelled of salt and fish. So hungry.

The old man moaned. A tear escaped his eyes.

This was wrong. I was a hunter. I was not a supernatural being. I didn't belong in this form. This wouldn't be my destiny. Not if I had any say about it.

"No," I said, weak but loud enough for Sotos to hear.

Sotos lifted his head from the man. "Then you will die."

"Then I die."

I gasped when a net sprawled across me.

"You cannot have her," Sotos hissed through his fangs as he leaped into the lake. The fisherman grabbed his paddle and started getting out of dodge.

"Start the engine, Oz!"

I was yanked off the canoe and into the lake. An engine roared and I was whipped through the water at breakneck speed.

Once the motor stopped at the pier, I was swiftly hauled up onto the motorboat. Through the net, I smiled at Blake and Oz. "You guys are awesome."

"Did you feed yet, my dear?" Oz asked, his glasses crooked on his nose.

"No way."

"Get her out of the net, my boy, and let's save our girl."

Blake cut the net away with a knife. "I thought I'd lost you, Jaz."

I swallowed hard. "Me too."

He glanced down at my tail. "Although, being mermaid becomes you, I want my Jaz back."

I flapped my tail. "I'm so ready to be back."

"Open wide, my dear." Oz held a blue vial.

I opened my mouth and he poured the liquid down my throat. I coughed. "Gross."

Nerves danced along my skin. "How long does this take? I think he's coming."

Blake stood, hands fisted. "He's not taking you again."

Something splashed out of the water behind Blake. It wasn't Sotos. A female mermaid with long blonde hair latched around his shoulders and pulled him into the lake.

"Amber!" She was a freaking mermaid!

Oz tossed me Blake's blade. "Save our boy, Jaz, before the serum returns your god-given legs."

I dove in after them.

I heard them at the very bottom of the lake.

Sotos and Amber were arguing. It was a language of sounds filled with hostility. Bits of pieces came to me. The two were cousins. Amber wanted Blake as her mate. The powerful mermaids could walk the lands. Sotos wanted to feed on him and kill him because I loved him.

Blake struggled between them. He would lose his breath soon.

Knife pointed toward them, I swam as quickly as possible. Sotos spotted me.

Jaz, put the knife down.

His power urged me to stop. I fought him as I neared them.

Jaz, stop!

Against my will, I halted between them, facing Blake.

Suddenly, Blake went still.

No, no, no!

I screamed. I screamed with all the pain and horror inside me. An underwater sound poured out of my mouth. Alien. Inhuman. So loud and painful even to my own ears. Sotos and Amber covered their ears and cried with me. As if they couldn't help themselves. As if I had power over them.

The knife was taken from my hand.

Blake was alive! He took the weapon and sliced at Sotos and then Amber. They scattered, blood trailing behind them.

I grabbed Blake's hand, and started toward the surface, but I felt the change. I rolled into myself as pain swirled up my body as if pulling me part.

Not yet, not yet.

No way to stop it. I was becoming human again.

My tail ripped apart. Blood and skin trailing around me. My legs formed.

Blake and I reached for each other and held on. I felt him go slack as I tried to kick up toward the surface but it was no use. I wasn't strong enough.

Something bright appeared from above us. A blue orb floated down from the surface—a magical life preserver from Oz. The orb formed around us and air filled my lungs. I gasped for breath. We began to move toward the surface.

Blake was still in my arms, unconscious. "Blake, wake up! Please!"

I slapped him. He gagged up lake water onto my chest.

Yeah, I was too happy to be grossed out.

He blinked his eyes. "We made it."

"We did."

"I thought I'd lost you."

"Not yet."

"Jaz." He pulled me to him. "I love you."

"W-What?" I reared back. Blake had fainted.

From the pier, we poured Oz's potion into the lake.

"So this will ward off merpeople from these waters?" Blake asked Oz.

"For the next century or so."

"Good. Um, Oz?" Blake scratched his neck.

"Yes, my boy."

"What I said to you before ..."

"No need, Blake. I know you were scared of losing our Jaz, and I hadn't been doing my job by you both. We're going to have to step up our training on many levels. Now, I must get back to Chapel Hill and get started on a new criteria."

Oz snapped his fingers and was gone.

"No fair he gets to do that," I said, looking out into

the lake.

Blake walked over to me. “How do you feel?”

“Normal, if you can believe that.” I took a big breath and turned to him. “Something happened down there while I was part fish.” Something I couldn’t explain. “For a brief moment, it was like I could control them.” I remembered their shocked faces, their distress that they couldn’t stop what was happening. “What do you think it means?”

“I don’t know. I’m just glad its over.”

He was right. Why worry about it now when there was something even more important to discuss. “Blake?”

“Hmm?” He slid his arms around my waist and pulled me to him.

“What you said in the orb ...”

“What’d I say?”

I met his confused eyes. “You don’t remember?”

“Tell me.”

“Never mind.” I looked away.

With his finger on my chin, he nudged me back. “Did it have to do with love?”

My eyes widened and he smiled. I shoved him. “It’s been three days!”

“What took *you* so long to bring it up?” He laughed. “You think I’d forget the first time I told my girl I loved her?” He leaned down and softly kissed me. “Not in this lifetime.”

I smiled, pulling him close. My chest ached, but this time with so much joy and love.

“It was the rainbow tail that lured you in, huh? Wasn’t it?”

Blake burst out laughing, and for the first time in a long while, I felt everything was just as it should be.

Midnight Troll

by Mari Hestekin

I'm warm, wrapped up in my dream. The sun shining, me and Robby on the porch. I'm playing video games, he's drawing the characters from my game—our favorite way to spend time. I see us as though I'm a bird, from above looking down on the happy sibling scene.

I feel a chill—looking up, I see the sun slide behind a cloud and then drop below the horizon like a coin in a slot. I am no longer a bird skimming above; I'm slammed back into my body on the porch. It's suddenly cold—I feel so cold—goose bumps break out on my body and my skin crawls. I hear a noise, a loud crash and a scream ... I can't move. I try to get up, to run, to freak out, but I'm locked in that dream state where you just can't budge. I turn to Robby.

"Rainey—"

And then I woke up, like I always do. Robby was trying to tell me—what? That it would be the last time I'd ever get to see him? I've been away for over a year and almost every night I dream, thinking about Robby, the last time I saw him or my parents—well, saw them alive any way. If only I could have moved to help them.

When the old car I was in rocked on its flattened tires, I realized those cries I heard weren't just in my dream—this was real. And something seriously wrong was going on out there.

Slowly, I scooted to the far side of the bench seat in the old Buick, away from the noises. After a string of too many nights spent in random doorways, the refuge of this dead-end street, the rotting upholstery in this abandoned car under a forgotten bridge was a welcome relief. Well, it should have been, anyway. Now it just felt like a cage. I preferred to avoid trouble, but trouble, once again, seemed to have found me. As the battle raged out in the dirty street, I tried to get out of this cage, any way I could.

I gently pushed on the door and when it squealed in resistance I paused. Oh crap; did they hear me? The struggle raged on, and the fighters seemed oblivious to the noise so I pushed it again and it stopped when it hit the crumbling bridge support, leaving me just enough room to squeeze out. As I crouched on the sticky blacktop, another crash rocked the car. I huddled behind the flattened tire. Now what? I was still trapped, out of the car but the only way to escape was through the struggle. I'd wait it out.

It was dark—really dark—on that street. I chose the car for that reason, thinking I could rest undetected, but being trapped never occurred to me. My skin crawled, just like it had all those nights in the doorways, just like it did in my dreams and I had that creepy feeling like something was watching me, something was not right.

SQWAK! The door I rested against just moments

before ripped open and a thick voice yelled "Where is she!?" It sounded like the speaker was yelling through a mouthful of pudding. Gross. Whoever that pudding mouth was, he was looking for me. My heart began to thud.

"No!" another voice yelled. I felt the car rumble as it shook, more struggling and the sound of something loud skidding across the ground. I reached down when it thunked against my shoe and found a heavy length of chain. It would have to serve as my protection.

There was a moment of silence and before I could think twice, I wrapped the end of the heavy chain around my hand, and jumped out from behind the car. I waved it in an arc in front of me with a wild scream, hoping to startle whoever was out there so I could make a break for it.

"Here!" a voice called. I turned and lashed the chain toward the voice and felt it connect with something. I looked down and saw it wrapped around the legs of the creature in front of me. But they weren't legs so much as they were really long, deformed arms, covered with ginger-colored hair that spread up over its shoulders, down its torso and up toward its head. Eyes like a reptile. Teeth like a shark. The chain held him immobile. Back legs, covered in khaki, flailed helplessly.

Suddenly, a person in black rushed up, giant knife flashing, and buried it in the back of the creature's neck. It dropped immediately with an inhuman squeal. I dropped too, as I backed away from the surreal scene, heels catching on the curb, landing flat on my behind before I could run.

The girl looked up, eyes gleaming. "Nice work! I'm Lauren." Lauren was dressed in head-to-toe black with a slicked-back blonde ponytail and gloved hands. "That your first one?" She asked as she extracted her knife with a quick jerk, wiping it on the back of the creature's pants and re-sheathing it.

My mouth snapped shut audibly. I hadn't realized it was open. "My ... first?"

Realization dawned on Lauren. "Oh, wow—you've never seen a troll before, have you?"

"A troll? A troll? What?" I shook my head, trying to make sense of the words but they continued to confuse me. I tried to sink down into my hoodie, looking down to make a curtain of dirty blonde between this surreal reality and me. What have I gotten myself into now?

"S'okay, sweetie," said Lauren, reassuringly. She may have murdered that thing but she wasn't going to hurt me. "What's your name?"

"Uh ... Rainey?"

"Rainey—I know it's a lot to take in. I just assumed you knew—I mean, he's been stalking you for like two weeks."

My jaw dropped open again. "Stalking ... me? Oh my god. I knew it! I felt it. Tingles. But—how? And why? And how do you know?"

"I know you're confused, but I'm on your side. I was tracking him and I found him stalking you. Every night. When you moved out here I thought you were luring him, trying to trap him."

"Luring him? Trapping him? For what?"

"To kill him."

We walked away from the dark street after pulling the hairy troll into the Buick and carefully torching it to erase the evidence and ensure the troll was dead. Lauren filled me in on the trolls she'd discovered, going a few years back. Like me, she lived where she could, was homeless. But unlike me, her first encounter left her with scars.

"You know that tunnel on the playground in the park on Morgan hill? That's where I was staying."

"Good cover. Out of the way." I made a mental note to add parks to my list of safe places to crash. "I've been on Duncan, hiding wherever I could until I tracked down this car. It was so out of the way—I thought it would be safe."

"You were smart to move. I got comfortable. Stayed like two weeks." We walked swiftly through the darkened streets, winding all around to throw off potential followers. "One of those things yanked me out of the tunnel by my feet. Almost knocked me out just from that."

"And it was a ... troll?" I didn't want to say the word. It sounded so crazy.

"Yeah, but I didn't know that—I didn't know *what* was going on. I fought and scratched and tried to get away. I drew blood and it scarred my fingers."

"How did you get away? Why was it coming for you? And why was it coming for me?"

"Best I can tell? Trolls hunt humans. Whole 'Circle of Life' sort of thing. Tonight it was hunting you, and back then it was hunting me. And someone had my back, just like I have yours. And now you can work with us to get the rest of them. We're hunting for their headquarters. RJ thinks we're close."

"RJ?"

"Yeah," said Lauren, purposefully turning corners, leading us somewhere in the night. "He saved me and Dexter—you'll meet them here."

Lauren stopped walking and I looked at the building before us. We were at the entrance to the Willow Street Rescue Mission. "No sleeping out here tonight, my friend. Come on—you can have my bed."

I dreamed again ... of sunshine ... laughter ... hugs ... soft pillows ... hot food ... love ... things that were few and far between in this reality, but the things that once filled my world. Me and Robby hanging out on the porch, doing our own thing. Then Robby looked up at me and smiled and said ...

"If she don't wake up, Imma take her toast."

"Uh, no you're not," said Lauren. "Or you'll answer to me."

I cautiously opened an eye and saw blue-jeaned knees standing next to a tray filled with food. The steam was still rising off a cup of strong-smelling coffee. I scrambled up and grabbed for the food, crunching on the fresh crisp toast next to the bacon, fruit and coffee. I sighed; this was better than any dream. The knees retreated with an audible sigh.

"I got you cream and sugar, didn't know how you took it," Lauren gestured to the coffee. "You crashed, hard. I knew you'd be hungry, and Matilda makes a mean breakfast. I didn't want to wake you—but I fear that douchebag Dexter beat me to it."

"Hey! Not nice!" said blue-jean knees. "I'm a growing boy." Dexter had folded up his sizeable frame and was lacing up his boots, two beds over.

"Thanks for your bed, Lauren." I gulped down the coffee that was hot enough to burn going down.

"No problem. RJ usually sleeps here, but he didn't come in last night. I crashed on his rack."

"Well, I appreciate it. It's been a while." I leaned back on the headboard, thankful for the warm food and soft bed. "Hey—Dexter? You want this?" I gestured to the toast left on my tray as he slung his backpack over his shoulder and moved for the door.

"Really? Yeah, thanks." I wrapped the two triangles and handed them over. As he walked off, I noticed the TV on the bookcase across the room. On it, I saw the husk of a burned-out car, crouched under a crumbled old bridge in a part of town where people don't visit.

The car where I had been last night.

The car I slept in before I helped kill the troll that was, right now, probably what was covered under that white sheet.

I saw the firemen, the police, the coroner and the reporters buzzing around. The red lights flashed, making it seem as though the car was still burning.

Lauren followed my intent gaze and grabbed the remote to turn up the volume as the reporter rambled on.

... police say the victim didn't have identification and there seems to be no motive. What they do know is that it was a man, between 35 and 50, who appears to

have been brutally beaten and stabbed before the car was set on fire ...

"That ..."

"Yes," said Lauren, muting the TV and checking to see if anyone else noticed anything out of the ordinary, but nobody else was paying attention.

Lauren filled me in on the rest of the story as we walked around the streets near the shelter. "Me, Dexter, RJ—we're the troll hunters. Dexter and RJ bailed me out at the park when I was attacked last year. Together, we've taken out seven trolls—eight including that one last night."

"Nobody knows where they come from?"

"No. All I know is they love the humans. Eat 'em like popcorn."

"Eww."

"Yeah, well."

We heard footsteps slapping the pavement behind us and spun around to find Dexter, out of breath and red-faced.

"Oh, dude." His words were choppy, he was struggling to catch his breath. "Bad. News. Really. Bad. News."

Lauren snorted, "Did you drop your toast?"

"RJ. Dude. They got him."

I had survived my attack last night, but RJ had not.

"Where?" Lauren was over her bout of laughter, her face grim and focused.

"Uh, that alley? South of Reynolds?"

My skin started crawling. "That's near the bridge—

the car."

"He's been going that way, tracking. I went to look for him this morning. I found his pack—and this," he said, holding up a bloodstained bandana to Lauren.

She groaned, taking the cloth and holding it to her heart. "What was he thinking!? He totally baited that troll."

"He gambled and lost," nodded Dexter. "Man, that sucks."

"But I got it—we—got it." Lauren brightened as she wrapped her arm around my neck.

"I still just don't get it. Trolls? Really. Trolls?"

Lauren nodded as Dexter rifled through RJ's pack. "Yup, that's what we call 'em. Don't know what they are or where they come from, but we know where they go when we're done. RJ knew the most. He saved us both."

"I'd never seen them before," agreed Dexter. "RJ saved my skin. We both saved Lauren. And he was probably trying to get to you last night. He was tracking you."

"RJ recruited us when he found us—they got his family, all but his sister." Lauren filled me in as Dexter looked on. "He's been on the streets trying to track down as many trolls as he could find. He taught us how to take them out—stab 'em in the neck, then burn 'em up—and run like hell."

"Why? How?" Instead of clearing things up, they were just confusing me even more.

"He said that his family were all troll hunters, had been for generations. But the trolls started to fight back, stalked his family, killed off everyone—that's what happened to his family. He's been out for blood ever since. Here! Take this. Answers." Dexter handed me an old cardboard-covered notebook with familiar-looking doodles covering the front. "It's RJ's notebook. He would never leave it behind."

I took it from him and felt the tingles I felt when I was in the car and the troll was after me, the ones I felt in my dreams. I flipped through pages covered, margin-to-margin, with intricate drawings of hellish scenes. Close-up sketches of creatures that looked like the troll we killed last night. Images of wounds that I could only imagine the trolls had inflicted.

"What *is* all this?"

Lauren pointed at an image. "That's the one that almost got me. RJ was like an awesome artist and he drew pictures of the trolls he had seen over the years, just from memory. He never let that book out of his sight."

I paged through the book and was assaulted by image after image of gruesome trolls, all shapes and sizes. When I came to the last page there was a drawing, but this one was different; this one was me.

And that's when I blacked out.

I'm warm, wrapped up in my dream. The sun shining, me and Robby on the porch. I'm playing video games; he's drawing the characters from my game—our favorite way to spend time. It was a mild summer night, no moon, plenty of bugs. I pretend not to hear the thick growling, the high, thin cries. But I can't

ignore the crash. I'm on my feet in a second. Robby looks over at me and with one final word—"Rainey"—pushes me off the porch, into the ravine that runs next to the house. I don't even scream. I don't know what was happening. I see a flash of claws and giant teeth as something crashes through the screen. The next thing I know, the police find me in the bushes. It's the next day. My parents were killed. There's no sign of Robby. I have no idea what happened.

"Rainey!" Lauren was shaking my shoulders. "Are you okay?"

Tears streamed down my face. "Robby," I said. "Robby!" Lauren and Dexter shared a confused look. "Robby—RJ—is my brother."

I filled them in on what I could remember and together we figured it out. The trolls had gotten my parents; Robby got away, but they found him. And they were looking for me next.

"How did you end up in that car last night, on the street—with us?"

"I was in foster care. They wanted to move me out of state to protect me. So I ran. I've been wandering around for a little over a year. I've been in town for like two months. I don't stay anywhere long."

Dexter was tearing apart Robby's backpack, looking for any more useful information. The ground around the pack became littered with the things my brother, the Troll Hunter, had used: a sharp, sheathed knife. A collection of pens, a few flashlights. Random batteries. Gum. An old, portable radio. A lighter. Can of lighter fluid. Granola bars. Empty water bottles. All that was left of his life. He pulled out a dirty, yellowed envelope from a rip deep in the lining. He handed it to me. I opened it and found newspaper clippings, from my parents' murder, from the investigation, from my disappearance.

Once again, I was crying. "Wow. Now I'm sure that's Robby's backpack. He was such a hoarder! He never gave up. How did he get away? And if he's a troll hunter, what does that make me?"

Lauren gave Dexter an uneasy glance. "Robby thought he was getting close to the main troll, like, headquarters or whatever. Maybe now you can help us find it?"

"I don't know anything about trolls. How can I help?"

"Well, right now you can help me pack this back up," said Dexter. "We need to get back for dinner. My stomach is totally growling."

"Dexter, really? Rainey just found out her brother is dead and all you can think of is food?"

He zipped everything back into the pack and handed it to me. "This is yours now."

I hugged it to me, pretending it was Robby, and he was telling me everything was going to be okay.

We got back in time to get a tray of hot food, scooped out for us by Matilda, the matronly woman who helped take care of the day-to-day operations of Willow Street. The shelter usually held about 25 people, but the beds were mostly empty, and aside from the three of us, there seemed to be only four others in the building and most of them just came for the food.

I slipped my bread over to Dexter' plate and he gave me a sheepish grin. We sat silently, each of us wrapped in our thoughts of what we'd learned. Once again, the news was on.

... *This just in: the body discovered badly beaten, brutally stabbed and burned last night has been identified as Rupert Vaughdean, a member of the board at the local Willow Street Rescue Mission, a non-profit* ...

I felt the hair on the back of my neck stand up. Lauren and I paused in our meals, staring at the news in shock.

"Lauren ..."

"Rainey." She grabbed my hand and squeezed hard, giving me the strength to turn off the tears threatening to spill. Looking for Dexter, I turned to see him standing with another man near the office door. I could see Dexter was upset, but I couldn't see the other man's face. As he turned toward us, the tingles I felt grew stronger. Who was that? He put his hand on Dexter's arm in a reassuring way and they shared a brief man-hug before walking across the room. I felt his eyes bore a hole through me as they approached.

"Lauren—Dexter just told me about RJ; I'm so sorry to hear about him. I know he was a good friend to you both."

Lauren looked sharply to Dexter for clarification. "I told him about the note we found—that RJ was going home."

"Yeah, it was time for him to go on." Though visibly relieved, it was difficult for Lauren to talk about. "I'm really gonna miss him."

The man turned to face me full on, sparks in his eyes blazing. “I don’t think we’ve met; I’m Don Moore. I run the Mission here.” He reached out to shake my hand and the alarm bells were clanging in my head and my skin felt like it was crawling with electricity. I shook his hand firmly, confused by my reaction.

“Rainey,” I mumbled.

Dexter piped in, “She just came in this week. We found her doorway surfing downtown.”

“You’ll be much safer here. No telling what’s lurking out there. I’m sure you saw what happened to my partner, Rupert.” His hand swept to the TV, which was showing close-ups of the charred remains of the car, surrounded by yellow crime scene tape and those little numbers on triangles marking points of interest. The reporter came on to talk about Rupert Vaughdean, showing pictures of his philanthropic involvement, pictures of him helping out, filling trays at the shelter. “You never know where danger lurks.”

Later that night as I crashed on my bed, Lauren bunking next to me, I paged through Robby’s notebook with a flashlight. It began to flicker but I didn’t want to stop. I was just reconnecting with my brother again. I pulled Robby’s backpack closer and dug through it until I found another flashlight. I turned it on and was disappointed; it seemed to be some kind of weird black light that I didn’t think would work very well for reading.

But when the black light hit the page, I gasped so loud it echoed across the nearly empty room.

Robby's black light uncovered writing ... tiny little writing like he used to do on his drawings, covering all the open space in between the images. Robby had been watching me from the beginning, following me from a distance the moment he pushed me off the porch: cheering me on and urging me to get out of foster care and away from danger, wanting me to be safe, even though it meant he couldn't get close to me.

His notes told the story, visible only with his black light. I paged through the drawings again and was shocked by the narrative that unfolded; what had been hidden in plain sight. I read about a history I knew nothing about: my sweet, old grandfather was a troll hunter. He tried to pass the duty to my father, but he wanted no part of it—he wouldn't fight. But Robby would. My grandfather taught Robby everything he knew until he died. Then Robby continued—until the trolls found my family.

His words started to swim on the page.

... trolls ... fierce ... stalking ... finding the bloodline .. will kill us all ... must find Rainey ... killed 47 of them ... found Dexter running from a troll and saved him just in time—my first save! ... random attacks decreasing—but what does that mean? ... We got 2 more last night! ... Lauren is with us now, got her in the park ... Lauren got another one, we used Dexter as bait ...

I read through the night, and Robby told me the story I needed to know. These trolls were stalking my family and now I was the only one left. On the page with the intricately drawn portrait of me, he wrote his final entry: "Think it's time to bring in Rainey! Chased off her stalker. Ran toward Willow Street. Saw him again, stalking around the shelter. Why?"

My mind raced as I put the pieces together. I slipped out of bed and shook Lauren to wake her.

"Lauren—Robby figured it out—the final troll ..."

"Is me." The thick voice behind me stopped me in my tracks. I hadn't heard Mr. Moore approach, and when I turned to face him, I could see his eyes changing ... his teeth multiplying ... his arms lengthening to reach the ground as thick, brown hair sprouted up over his upper body. He rolled his shoulders as he completed his troll-transformation.

"Why are you doing this?" I backed away, moving slowly toward the door, trying to draw him away from the sleeping Lauren and Dexter.

"Oh, it's such good fun! The stalking. The killing. What more perfect cover than a *homeless* shelter? Who's going to miss the missing when they go missing?" He laughed like a maniac at his own cleverness. "And you came to me ... you jumped right into my web! First your brother and now you. I've already killed him, and now, once I get you out of the way, there will be no more pesky challenges to our authority."

I tried to stay calm, but just wanted to keep him distracted until I could figure out what to do next. "Why—I've never wanted to hurt you. I'll go away, I'll leave you alone! I'll pretend I never heard of trolls before. Why kill me?"

"Why me?" he mimicked me in a singsong falsetto. "Why me? Oh, poor me." His laughter stopped. "No! Poor ME! You have to pay the price. I've been waiting two hundred years to fulfill this payment. Your family killed my kind. You tracked us. Mercilessly. Strived to eradicate us. So we fought back! It's finally down to you. Your family took what is mine. And now? I take you."

My back was against the wall now—literally. I heard a noise behind me to the left and through the pass-through to the kitchen, out leapt a second troll. Matilda, recognizable now only by her purple stretch pants and the pearls that still circled her hairy, transformed neck. The trolls keened a strange noise to one another and Matilda joined Mr. Moore, both advancing on me.

Mr. Moore leapt forward and I jogged right to get out of his way. Those shark teeth nipped my shoulder and I cried out as I felt the burn from his acid mouth sink deeper in. It felt like those teeth were still digging in with the poison left behind.

He spun around when he heard Matilda cry out. Lauren and Dexter were standing behind us, weapons at the ready, advancing on the she-troll.

"You'll take nothing," Lauren said, flashing the length of chain in her hands that she had just used to strike Matilda.

Matilda charged at Lauren and she swung the chain to capture her freakish troll arms, but the troll grabbed the chain and pulled Lauren forward, pinning her to the ground. Dexter rushed Mr. Moore with the knife, but the troll anticipated it and swept out his arm to claw him aside. Dexter slid across the floor and hit his head on a table leg as the knife clattered away. I was momentarily forgotten as the trolls dealt with my friends. I racked my brain, trying to think of what to do next.

And then I remembered: a knife to the back of his neck, just like Lauren did when she took out that troll coming after me. I could do this. I slid to the left to get Dexter' knife as the troll advanced on Lauren. She was making her way up Lauren's body, using the chain to hold her down and whispering threats in her creepy pudding-thick voice. I crept up behind them and felt the weight of the knife in my hand. I thought about my parents. I thought about Robby. And before I could think anything else, I jumped on the troll's back and plunged the knife into her neck so deep the tip of it came out the front and nicked Lauren's shoulder as she slumped forward onto her.

Lauren bucked and I heaved to push Matilda out of the way. Across the room, Dexter was trying to hold off Mr. Moore. Lauren grabbed Dexter's knife from Matilda's neck and threw it across the room. He spun around, eyes shocked and slumped to the floor.

"Whoa," said Dexter, shaken and bleeding, but fine. "What the hell just happened?"

"Robby's notebook explained it all," I said as I removed the knife from the troll's neck, wiping it on his pants before handing it to Dexter. "It was him all the time—Mr. Moore? He was the, like, head troll around here."

"And Matilda, she was working with him and Rupert—they were all in on it."

"I'll get a first aid kit," said Lauren. "Dex, you've got some nasty scratches."

"Nothing I can't survive," he said. "The troll was

trying to eat my fingers. But I saved them." He wiggled them as proof.

"There's nobody left in the building," Lauren said when she returned with the first aid kit. "What the hell happened to everyone else?"

"Ouch!" said Dexter as Lauren wiped an antiseptic pad along the cuts on his arm. "There have been fewer people every day. I guess that's how the trolls kept up their strength?"

Together we cleaned out the kitchen of food and the office of cash. Dexter brought out a small bottle of lighter fluid from his backpack, Lauren handed him her lighter. We worked together to bolt the doors, lighting the building and torching the trolls inside before sneaking off into the dark night.

From the playground on the hill a few blocks away, we watched the shelter burn.

"Well, now what do we do?" Asked Lauren.

"Let's head south," said Dexter with a smile. "I hear the beaches are nice. We can look for a place to crash down there for a while."

It sounded great. But I knew it wasn't over. I knew I had to continue to figure out how to beat the trolls. I knew if any more of them existed, it would be up to me to find them—before they found me.

We heard the sirens approaching and saw the spotlights as the choppers flew overhead. We heard the breaking news on the radio from Robby's backpack about the shelter burning, speculating on what could be happening at Willow Street, and when would it end?

We didn't hear the crash of the shelter door leading to the alley. We didn't see the car, headlights off, creep away from the building. And we didn't hear the troll driving away, scarred and singed from fire, vowing his revenge.

Spectral Media

by Aaron Smith

When Alicia had nowhere else left to go, she went to see Daniel. He was her last resort. She knew his place well and it held fond memories, but it seemed like an eternity since she'd been there.

She climbed the stairs that led up to the small balcony on the back of the house and cautiously knocked on the door that led directly into Dan's room. Being there made her nervous.

When Dan saw Alicia, he immediately slammed the door in her face. Alicia was stunned but not really surprised. She trembled, but knocked again.

"What do you want?" Dan asked icily, opening the door a second time. He looked past her, down at the driveway, scanning the bushes that bordered the asphalt as if he suspected an ambush.

"Dan, I need help."

He started to close the door again. He wanted to shut it and hear the boards creak as she went away, but he couldn't do it. The way she had said "help" was so sincere, coming from such a deep place, that he had to know what had brought her to his door. He swung it open all the way.

"You're alone."

"Yes, Dan, I'm alone. Can I please come in?"

"Whatever," Dan said. He stepped aside, watched her walk in. Alicia wore a sweater to fight off the autumn chill, with blue jeans and knee-high leather boots that looked expensive. Her stylish attire was a contrast to Daniel's grungy faded jeans and old Led Zeppelin t-shirt.

Alicia looked around the room. Computer, bookshelves, a heap of laundry on the floor—the place was a mess.

"I haven't been here in ages, Dan."

"Why would you be?"

"We're friends."

"No, Alicia, we're not. We used to be, a long time ago."

"Whoever said we weren't anymore?"

"It didn't have to be said. It just went that way. What do you want?"

She sat down on the edge of Dan's unmade bed. Her face twisted and reddened, about to flood with tears. Dan stood and stared at her.

She hesitated, blinked a few times, refused to let the crying start, finally spoke.

"My whole life is falling apart."

Dan sighed. "Don't exaggerate. What happened? Did some guy turn you down for once? Did you lose your four hundred dollar purse?"

Alicia stood up, took a step forward, and slapped Dan across the face. Then she cried. Her whole body shook as she sat back down on the bed. Dan rubbed his cheek for a second, looked around for a tissue that didn't exist, grabbed a shirt that he thought might be clean, and handed it to her.

"Dan, please don't talk to me like that. You're the only one I have left. I can't go anywhere else. They're all against me now."

He couldn't stay mad at her. The stinging in his cheek was gone already and he looked at her and no longer saw the companion who had drifted away from him somewhere in the midst of high school and joined those who coveted popularity with an intensity that reached into ruthlessness. Instead, he saw the young girl he had confided in when they were innocent and still full of the joy and wonder that faded as they aged. They hadn't talked in a long time. They hadn't been friends now for several years, but deep down, they were the same two kids who loved one another. He still cared about her, in some part of his heart.

"Crap," he muttered as he sat down beside her, let her tears wet his shoulder. "I'm listening."

Alicia let it all out. The words flew like an endless flock of gulls sent spiraling skyward in a panic by a lighthouse foghorn.

"Two days ago I was away at school. High school ended perfectly, graduation was great and summer was amazing. I got to college right when I was supposed to and that first month was exactly how I imagined it. Everything was going great ... and then it all fell apart! It's like the whole world changed overnight.

"My friends turned against me all at once, Dan. Not just some of them, not just the ones at school but the old ones too, the ones from home and from high school. Things were said, mean things. Heather called me a slut, accused me of trying to steal her boyfriend—and I don't even *like* her boyfriend! My professors started intentionally embarrassing me in class, one called me a stupid cow. I went home for the weekend and my parents wouldn't let me in the house and they wouldn't even tell me why. So I went to my sister's place, begged her to let me crash there for a few days 'til I figured out what was wrong with everybody. She slammed the door in my face, like you did when I got here—except she didn't open it again. I even called Steven but he wouldn't even talk to me. Steve and I were supposed to stay friends. We only broke up because we were going to school so far apart, but he acted like he didn't want to know me ever again.

"I've called or gone to see thirty people in the past few days—I thought they cared about me. Friends, relatives, and the people I used to work with at the shoe store in the mall—even my old teachers. They all acted like I had the *plague* or something. The way they sounded on the phone or how they looked at me, it was like absolute hatred. I stayed in a damn hotel last night, alone! My car's out on the street and I'm terrified that any moment my dad will show up and take it away because it's in his name. I have a suitcase of clothes in the trunk and a little bit of money and my phone with nobody to call ... and that's all I have. I can't go back to school, can't go home, and can't find anybody to help me understand what happened to my life!

"Dan, it feels like my whole world has been ripped to shreds and my soul's been scraped raw. I don't understand this."

Alicia stopped talking, sobbed into the shirt.

Daniel stood up, began to pace. He tried to absorb

what he had just been told. His feelings were divided. After she had so easily turned her back on their friendship years ago, he was happy to see her knocked down a peg. Part of him smiled at her pain, thought maybe she deserved some of it, but that part was overruled quickly. Nobody deserved to cry like that. He shoved the feelings aside and tried to think without emotion. She *still* meant something to him—after all they had been through as kids, he knew she always would.

What could cause every person in someone's life to turn against them simultaneously? Daniel loved big questions, embraced puzzles. That's why he had been so unpopular once high school started and everybody divided up into their little cliques. He didn't fit any group. He thought too much, was too philosophical and ignored the petty stuff everybody else seemed to worry about all the time. But now he stood there, looking at someone who had turned her back on him not very long ago, and knowing he could not do the same to her.

"Alicia, I have to ask. I'm sorry. What did you do to make enemies so fast? Something had to have started this."

She looked up. "Dan ... no. I've pissed people off before, okay? Yeah, my parents have been mad at me when I did something stupid and Heather and I have blowouts all the time because sometimes best friends fight and yes, teachers have been mad at me for saying some smartass comment in class ... but this is beyond all that. It's like I'm a leper or something. It's so bad that I'm amazed you haven't thrown me out yet."

"I can't," Dan said. "This is much too interesting."

"That's cruel."

"Sorry, didn't mean it that way. I just love a mystery. Can I see your phone?"

"Why?"

"Well I assume there are texts on it, right?"

"Yes."

"From people you've tried to contact since this mess began?"

"Yeah, you're right," Alicia said as she fished her phone from her purse, brought the saved texts up on screen and surrendered it to Dan.

"Geez, Alicia," Dan said, "how much do you text?"

"About the same amount as anybody else; it's the way we all communicate now. Don't you?"

"Not if I can help it. I hate it. It's almost impossible to communicate anything meaningful in short, abbreviated phrases. And it kills people's abilities to use real words, real sentences."

"Well it works for most of us."

"I can see that. Now give me a minute to read these."

Alicia watched as Dan scrolled down the long list of texts, stopping for a second to digest each one, his facial expressions going from a look of surprise to a scowl to a red mask of real anger.

"Unbelievable!" Dan said as he tossed the phone onto the bed as if it had burned his hand. "You weren't kidding. The messages ... they're venomous. And you didn't do anything to initiate this?"

"No, Dan, I told you I didn't."

"Swear to it."

"I'm serious, Dan. Fine, I swear I didn't do

anything to anybody. Even if I did, how could I turn so many people against me at the same time?"

"That's my question, too. Do all these people even know each other?"

"No, not even close. My professors know me as a new student this year, my relatives have known me my whole life, my friends from high school are a whole different group and they don't all know my parents, and the people I worked with at the mall don't know my parents or my teachers. It's like all the aspects of my life just collided and everybody started to hate me at the same time, but what can trigger that? Where's the common ground?"

"Alicia, listen. I'm having a thought, but it's a little crazy. I need to think about this, and I need to be alone."

"You're throwing me out too?"

"No, I'm not turning against you, not like them. Trust me. Just leave for a while, a few hours."

Dan looked at the clock on the wall. It was two in the afternoon. He picked up his wallet from the dresser, took out thirty dollars, handed it to Alicia. "Take this and go see a movie or something. Go alone. Don't call anybody or try to see anyone. Come back at six—maybe I'll have this figured out by then."

Alicia took the money, stared hopefully at Dan for a second. "Thanks."

Dan listened as Alicia's boots pounded down the outside stairs. He heard her start her car and drive away. He thought about how ridiculous his idea was, but he could find no other explanation.

One thing Alicia had said kept ringing in Dan's

mind.

It's like all the aspects of my life just collided.

That was the key to the whole mess, Dan suspected. He could think of only one place where every piece of a person's life and experiences was lumped together in one mass of memories and time periods. He sat down at his computer to see where his theory would lead.

Six o'clock arrived and Dan was convinced he was right. His mother called him downstairs for dinner and he made the excuse of being exhausted. He hoped his parents would be too busy eating to hear Alicia return if she did.

She came back at six-thirty.

"How do you feel?" Dan asked as he let her in.

"I don't even remember the movie. I feel like I don't exist anymore. Everything I was is gone."

"That's not true. You're real." He reached out to touch her arm. "See? You're still solid. Sit down."

She sat on the bed. "Can I stay here tonight? Will your parents mind?"

"We'll worry about that later if we have to. Let's see if we can fix things first. Just relax."

Alicia pulled her boots off, swung her legs up onto the bed, leaned back against the pillows and closed her eyes. "I'm so tired."

"Don't go to sleep," Dan said. "Just listen. If this starts to sound too crazy, tell me to shut up; but this is starting to make sense in a very strange way."

"I'm listening."

"Okay, here goes. You said it felt like all the

different aspects of your life collided, like separate pieces of your world had all ganged up on you, right? Well there *is* a place where everybody who suddenly seems to hate you is connected. I double-checked. They're all on your friends list on Facebook."

"So what if they are?" Alicia asked. "Everybody has a mixed-up list like that."

"Yes, but not everybody goes through what you're going through right now. I'm not on that list and whatever happened to all those people obviously hasn't happened to me."

"But *what* happened, Dan? You're not making sense yet!"

"Well this is where it gets weird."

"Just say it!"

"I read an article a while ago, a philosophical piece by a professor of theology. He was disturbed by the amount of time people spend interacting through technology now: the Facebook and Twitter activity, the fact that people never seem to put down their phones, the way people cross the street without even looking up because their texting is too important to interrupt even for the sake of safety. He wrote that it seemed to him that phones and computers had become an extension of the body and our online identities had become, in a manner of speaking, extensions of our souls.

"For many people today, having their means of constant communication taken away would literally hurt them! Rather than using technology as a tool, people are letting technology control them. Did you know that half the brides in the United States over the past two years updated their relationship statuses within ten minutes of exchanging vows? That statistic frightens me.

"Social media is becoming like a religion—a *cult*. People's lives revolve around it as if it's as important as their health or their money or their God. Am I making any sense, Alicia?"

"Yes ... but I still don't see how that has anything to do with me. Yes, okay, we're addicted to phones and Facebook, but how does that connect to my situation?"

Dan paused. He weighed his next words carefully, knowing Alicia would likely think he'd gone over the edge.

"I'm talking about a modern equivalent of what used to be called ghosts—or maybe demons."

Alicia sat straight up at those words, her eyes open and disbelief on her face. "This is not a joke, Dan!"

"Hold on," Dan said in a voice meant to soothe. "Let me explain."

"Okay."

"The thing is, Alicia, stories about spirits about entities invading people's bodies or souls or homes have shown up in every culture in human history, so maybe there has to be something to it, even if it's not really what it seems to be on the surface. So maybe, if humanity's evolved into such a technological society, the things that go bump in the night are evolving too. In the twenty-first century, if something evil wanted to hurt you, what better way would it have than to attack you through your home and your family, and maybe your online soul and the people connected to it are easier for such an entity to get at. So it attaches itself to you and spreads from person to person as communication takes place in cyberspace, sending all that negative energy right back at you."

"Dan, you're saying I have a demon that acts like a computer virus?"

"In theory, yes, I think so."

"How do you even come up with an idea like that?"

"You know how I am, Alicia, or at least you used to know me. I'm a thinker. I think a lot and I connect ideas and I do come up with crazy ideas. You used to appreciate that aspect of me. Anyway, can you think of a better explanation?"

"No."

"I didn't think so."

"So what can we do about it? We can't just call a priest and ask him to exorcise my phone and my Facebook, can we?"

"I think I can deal with it."

"What are you thinking?"

"I'll sign up for Facebook and you can send me a friend request to get me into this mess."

"Dan, won't that turn you into one of them? You'll be an Alicia-hating zombie like everybody else in my life!"

"No, I don't think I will. I think I can fight it. I might even be immune."

"Why would you be any different?"

"Because I don't care about the things everybody else cares about. My phone is something I use when I need to make a call. I use my computer for research or entertainment–not socializing. I have no interest in being part of the Facebook flock. I don't Tweet. And you should know if you have any understanding of me left after all the time we didn't talk, that I really don't care what most people think about me. I don't follow trends or worry about popularity. I listen to the music I like because I *like* it, not because Billboard tells me to. I wear these clothes because they feel *comfortable*, not because I want to fit some clique. I think on my own terms, Alicia. I'm not part of the herd. Let this thing that's been bothering you try to eat me like it's eaten the souls of everybody else on that stupid list. I'll give it a piece of my mind and I think it'll find me pretty hard to swallow."

Alicia laughed. "You're really sure of yourself, aren't you?"

"Yes, I am," Dan said, "because I know exactly who I am. I'm not as defined by the people around."

"Like I am." Alicia looked defeated.

Dan reached out for her arm again. "Are you ready to do this?"

She hesitated. "Not yet, Dan. Soon, but can you just sit with me for a while?"

"Alicia, wake up. It's time."

Dan had let her fall asleep while he sat thinking, preparing. It was now ten. Alicia opened her eyes, stretched.

"Here," Dan handed her the phone. "Give me a minute and we'll do this."

"Are you sure?"

"There's no other option."

Dan created a Facebook account, just his name and a picture.

Alicia accessed her account on her phone. "Okay, I've found you. Should I do it?"

"Go," Dan said.

A minute passed as Alicia manipulated the options on the small screen.

On Dan's monitor, the little red activity icon at the top of the Facebook page appeared.

One new Friend Request.

"I'm accepting it now," Dan said. "Put your boots back on. If anything crazy happens, be ready to run."

On the screen, the tiny text bubble announced that Daniel and Alicia were now friends. It was absurd, Dan thought, that after being so close as kids, then drifting so far apart, that a crisis revolving around a website suddenly seemed to be bringing them back together. As that thought crossed Dan's mind, the world around him shimmered and melted away and he was alone, in a place that felt like a dream.

In an instant, he was surrounded by a crowd of people, stretching as far as he could see. They were packed tightly together and the air was full of energy, emotion and noise. Dan could feel hate in the atmosphere, perhaps even violence about to erupt. Dan struggled to focus his vision on the faces of those surrounding him. Many were strangers to him, but he began to see a few he recognized.

He spotted Alicia's family; her mother, her sister. They were shrieking like banshees when he saw them, as if possessed by some force that controlled the entire scene.

He saw a few familiar faces from the childhood he and Alicia had shared. Ms. Brant, their second grade teacher looked down on him with a threatening expression. Dan realized that she shouldn't be so tall, not anymore; he wasn't his second-grade size now. With that thought, the intimidating woman shrank, or Dan grew taller, or both—and they were face to face.

"Ms. Brant? What is this place?"

"Don't ask stupid questions, Daniel! Think before you speak! We can't waste any more time. We must punish her!"

"Ms. Brant, wait a minute. You may have scared me when I was 7, but not anymore. Can you please tell me what's going on here?"

"That wicked girl must be finished. We must make her destroy herself."

"There has to be a reason, Ms. Brant. This doesn't make sense. Just tell me why."

Dan didn't get an answer. The crowd moved and he was swirled away from the teacher and spun around and pulled further into the chaos.

He gathered all his energy and shouted, loud and furious. Trying to cut through the thick noise, he cried out, "Everybody shut up now!"

Somehow, it worked. The crowd parted, backed away from Dan, forming an immense circle with him alone in the middle.

"Ha!" someone shouted. "We have a new one and he doesn't get it. He needs to be enlightened. Who'll do the honors?"

"I will," said a female voice. "I know this one."

Dan watched as Heather stepped out of the crowd, came toward him. She was, or had been, Alicia's best friend for years now, probably all through high school.

Everyone expected the two girls to remain inseparable for life.

"What's up, weirdo?" Heather said coldly. She and Dan had never gotten along—he just wasn't cool enough for her. Dan remembered how he felt when Alicia chose Heather over him, but he saw the decision as Heather's doing, not Alicia's fault. "Why don't you tell me?" Dan countered. "None of this is right, none of this is real. I think all you people have gone insane."

"Oh no," Heather said with an icy sneer, "we're the ones who see reality. We know *exactly* what she is and what has to be done. Why don't you help us, Dan? You have reasons to want her gone as much as we do."

"What about you, Heather? Do you even understand your reasons, or are you just swept up in the wave—you and everybody else, with your minds stuck here and confused by some situation you can't understand?"

"Dan, you have it reversed," Heather said, and a frozen smile came across her face. "You're the one who doesn't understand. Let me help you."

She kissed him. She leaned forward, reached up, grabbed the back of Dan's head by the hair, and pulled him forward, kissed him hard. Their lips locked and Dan felt Heather's tongue meet his. He lost all his thoughts in the moment, his identity absorbed in the mass of emotions that guided the whole of the crowd. He could hear them now, clearly, without interference from his own thoughts. He began to communicate with the rest of the entity, joined the chorus of hate.

Dan had not spoken since answering the Friend Request. He had not moved. Alicia watched as he sat, still and silent, in front of the computer. She waited and grew more afraid with each new moment of nothing.

"Dan?"

No response.

"Dan?" she tried again.

He didn't move.

"Daniel!" she cried out in desperation, not caring if his parents downstairs heard.

He moved then. His head began to turn toward Alicia. They made eye contact and Alicia could see that everything had changed. She began to shake again.

Dan stood up, fast and violent. The chair toppled over behind him and he growled inhumanly. Alicia moved over further on the bed, putting distance between them.

Dan stared hard at her for a moment, swaying back and forth as if dazed. He began to move forward, a stumbling awkward motion, like something from a Frankenstein movie. He stretched out his arms, collided with the edge of the bed, toppled forward and fell onto her. His hands went to her throat and he began to squeeze.

Alicia was terrified. Dan was much stronger than her. She couldn't breathe. Tears welled up in her eyes. She tried to scream but couldn't find the air. Dan didn't speak, but the intensity in his eyes told her he was trying to kill her.

She made one desperate move to save herself, brought her knee up, fast and ruthless, into Dan's crotch. It was the first time in her life she had struck anyone like that. The impact was strong and the hands around her throat released. Dan howled out in pain, lifted his head and jerked back in reaction to the pain. She put her hands against his chest, shoved him away. He fell off the bed, hit the floor, and lay there dazed, staring up at the ceiling with a blank face.

Alicia crawled over to the edge of the bed, looked down at Dan. "Oh my God, oh my God, oh my God ..."

Dan's mind spun around and around. He tried to focus his vision. He was back in the other place now. Alicia was gone and he was surrounded by the crowd: Heather and Ms. Brant and the rest. They stared at him with zombie eyes.

"Go back! Finish her! Destroy her and set us free!"

"No," Dan shouted. He was wracked with guilt for what he had almost done to Alicia. His thoughts were chaos and it was harder and harder to tell what was real. His physical body was in pain, he didn't want to go back, but the longer he stayed here, the more dangerous the situation would become.

But he could still hear Alicia. Somehow, the voice with which she spoke in that world echoed in his brain. He heard her crying.

"Dan ... I'm so sorry! Dan?"

He had almost killed her and still, she cried for him. What choice did she have? He had been her last hope, the life raft she prayed would carry her through the storm.

These others, Dan thought as he looked at the faces around him, hate her because they're expected to.

They're caught up in the crowd, emotions gone viral. I'm better than that. I hate what I hate because I have reason to—not because it leads to acceptance. Yes, I've hated Alicia at times. She hurt me, she threw me away. But that's part of growing up. Sometimes people drift apart. It happens. Get over it, Dan!

"Who's in charge of you animals?" Dan shouted at the souls around him. "Who's pulling the strings, you pathetic puppets? It's not you, Heather. You were never smart enough for that! Can't you people see you've given up your freedom? Who's running the show? Show yourself!"

The crowd slowly disappeared. For a moment, Dan was alone. He waited.

The air in that empty realm began to sizzle. Dan's mind began to hurt, like being scalded by invisible fire. The pain was accompanied by laughter that seemed to come from all around.

"Show yourself!" Dan shouted again.

He was no longer alone. Alicia was there, or at least what appeared to be Alicia. It looked like her, but the presence felt wrong to Dan. He had known Alicia since they were 5, and this was *not* her.

"Daniel," it said, and it spoke with Alicia's voice. "You know what you want to do to me. You remember how I hurt you. You have a chance now, an opportunity to make things even. You're closer to me, in both worlds, than all those others. I'm right here, Daniel. Go back to your body and finish what you started."

"You're not Alicia," Dan said. He was calm now, certain. "She doesn't talk like that. Those aren't the words she'd choose. You can fool those other people, but not me. You see, I don't care about being part of a flock, doing what everybody else is doing, mindless following. I am who I am—I'm not who anybody wants me to be."

"But how do you know, Daniel, that I'm not the true Alicia? Maybe I came to you for help just to pull you into this, to get you to do what you know you want to do to me."

"Then prove to me that you're her. You've taken over the minds of all these people, all of Alicia's friends, but you haven't taken over *her* mind. Maybe you can't see through to her thoughts, her memories. Tell me this: when Alicia and I were 7, we played in the woods behind my grandmother's house. We pretended we were pioneers out in the wilderness. But what did we call ourselves?"

There was no reply, only silence. The thing that looked like Alicia just stood there. Dan moved, wondering how solid his body was in this ethereal place, and got his answer when his fist connected with the thing's face. It shattered into a burst of gray mist, but did not disperse. The cloud hung there and moved closer, faster than it should have been able to. Dan was enveloped, he could feel the electrical heat of the cyber-demon, emotions that were more programming than actual feeling sizzling around him—trying to penetrate his mind. It was pure hate, stronger than anything Dan had experienced before. Fear filled him, then anger. He knew suddenly, with no doubt, that if he allowed the demon to overwhelm him there, in the world of data, that his soul would not go back to his body. Alicia would be left there with something comatose or maybe even dead. He tried to get out of the cloud. It seemed to have no boundaries, seemed to go on forever.

"Let me out!"

"You are part of me now, Daniel."

"But you're not real."

"I am information. Nothing is more real than that."

"That's bull!" Dan shouted. "Without something to represent, information is meaningless. My name is a piece of information, and it means something because *I* am real! You need to control people, because outside of your pathetic little world of bits and bytes, you do not exist! So you looked like Alicia, and then you looked like this cloud of energy—but they're all masks. Why don't you show me what you really are?"

"As you wish."

The cloud vanished. A parade of faces filled the space around Dan, a panorama of hurt and betrayal and devastation. Some cried, some stared in disbelief. Dan wondered who they were—then he understood. The angles from which they looked at him made him understand. He was looking out from the inside of computer monitors and smart phones. They were the faces of those who had been broken by the demon that now toyed with Alicia—and wanted to absorb him.

"Nice view, isn't it?" the demon taunted.

Dan said nothing. He closed his eyes and brought an image up in his mind. A keyboard. He imagined his fingers coming down on the keys in three places. *Ctrl-Alt-Delete.* He saw what he wanted to see and chose to believe. A window popped up. He saw the *End Program Now* button depress. He felt the energy around him weaken. He opened his eyes.

Dan stood alone now among nothingness, but there was still sound. He heard the voice, starting out like Alicia's and growing into something else, something distant and harsh, as the words came out.

"Close one door ... and I'll find another. There are more of *them* than there are of *you*, Daniel. And they're all connected because they want to be. This is not over."

"It is for now," Dan said to the emptiness, and he willed his mind back to his body.

Dan woke to a persistent buzzing. He moaned. His body ached. He sat up, looked around. He was still on the bedroom floor. Alicia was sitting on the bed, her phone in hand, running her finger across the touch screen. She heard Dan move, looked down at him.

"Don't ..."

"I won't, Alicia," Dan said, rubbing the back of his head. "I don't think I can even stand. I'm ... I'm sorry about ..."

"It's okay. Are you all right?"

"I think so. I'm just sore. What are you doing?"

The phone was vibrating in Alicia's hand.

"It won't stop! One text after another; they keep coming. They're all apologizing! I don't understand what happened."

"I don't think you should worry about it anymore. Everything's fine now. Trust me."

"I don't know what to say, Dan."

"Alicia," Dan said as he struggled to his feet with a groan and sat down beside her on the bed, "do you remember when we used to play in the woods when we were kids?"

"We lived in our imaginary cabin. We pretended to be pioneers, Martha and Abraham. Wow, that was a long time ago! Funny how clear those memories seem."

"Yeah. I remember how we were back then, too—but I don't know anything about you now. Can you put the phone down for a while? The texts can wait. Maybe we can just talk."

Alicia stayed until well after midnight. She and Dan were close again, almost as if no gulf had ever grown between them. They remembered the old times, laughed a lot, cried a little and made plans for the future together.

When Dan woke up at seven, he missed her. He showered, dressed, sat down and turned the computer on. There was an email with no subject line and a series of symbols where the name of the sender should have been, like the way swearing was disguised in old comic strips. He almost deleted it, but the email popped open when his mouse hovered over it.

"Daniel, I suppose you'll never sign on to Facebook again. I wouldn't if I were you. But don't worry; you'll hear from me again. You see, everything really is *connected. Everything! When you decide to go back to school, remember that your transcripts are stored on a network. And that driver's license that's so important to you: think about what runs the Department of Motor Vehicles. Arrest warrants, tax records, medical history, phone charges ... everything is connected, Daniel. Don't ever forget that. In my*

world, navigating through data is as easy as walking from room to room in a house in your world. I was only having a little fun with your friend, but you've upped the stakes, Danny Boy! Just wait until next time!"

Author Bios

All of these authors, with the exception of Mari Hestekin, contributed short stories to our *Prom Dates to Die For* anthology. If you liked *Something Wicked*, we hope you'll seek out *Prom*.

Lena Brown ("Arach War") used her characters from *Goddess Sisters,* her upcoming mythology series set at the fictional Mid America University, to create the creepy spidey tale. She's a wife, den mom, dance mom and coffee lover. Follow her on Twitter @lenabrownbooks. Lena Brown is the YA pen name for women's fiction author Malena Lott.

Heather Dearly ("Through a Glass Darkly") is published in short fiction with Nodin Press, and has authored even shorter non-fiction with the Six-Word Memoir® series. She's also the Assistant Editor at Book End Babes. An actress by training, and a stay-at-home mom by choice, she writes at her residence in Oklahoma where she lives with her husband and three children. She is currently working on a young adult novel. For more information, please visit her web site at www.trulymadlydearly.com.

Mari Hestekin ("Midnight Troll") is a long-time lover of words. This is her fiction debut, and she hopes to revisit the world of Rainey to bring her on more adventures. She was inspired to write about trolls because she feels they are an underserved supernatural demographic. Mari lives and writes with her husband and two children, who supply no shortage of drama from which to pull stories.

Kelly Parra's earliest stories were told with paintbrushes, but upon discovering the drama and forbidden love of romance and suspense novels, those paintbrushes were replaced with a keyboard. Now a multi-published author, our "Mermania" contributor has created memorable characters such as a graffiti artist, a psychic teen, and a tough undercover narc. A two-time RITA finalist, she divides her time between her novels, freelance writing, and the adventures of motherhood, where she juggles her home life with two children, a tattooed husband, and a sweet poodle. Visit her website www.kellyparra.com.

Jenny Peterson ("Under Loch and Cay") is a former lifestyle editor and current freelance writer living in Denver, CO. For her day job, she's had the opportunity to write about everything from her love of *Harry Potter* to local shopping. Her short fiction has appeared in anthologies such as Buzz Books' *Sleigh Ride*. Jenny spends most of her free time reading and writing YA fiction.

Aaron Smith ("Spectral Media") is the author of the science-fantasy novel *Gods and Galaxies,* the mystery novel *Season of Madness,* and many short stories including three featuring Sherlock Holmes. News about his work can be found at his blog at www.godsandgalaxies.blogspot.com

Did you enjoy *Something Wicked*? Why not try *Prom Dates to Die For?* Five paranormal tales set on Prom night More wicked fun.

www.ingramcontent.com/pod-product-compliance
Lightning Source LLC
LaVergne TN
LVHW091002080826
845145LV00003B/1102

* 9 7 8 1 9 3 8 4 9 3 0 6 5 *